# JOURNEY'S END

## AN OREGON TRAIL WESTERN ADVENTURE
## THE SLADES – BOOK 3

William Tresler

Copyright © 2021 by William Tresler.



**Publisher's Note**: This is a work of fiction. Names, characters, places and incidents are a product of the author's imagination. Locales and public names are sometimes used for atmospheric purposes. Any resemblance to actual people, living or dead, or to businesses, companies, events, institutions, or locales is completely coincidental.

# Contents

# Chapter 1
# Gyorgyike

"Gyorgyike! The master wants you!" The shrill call cut through Gyorgyike Szarka's consciousness like a death knell.

The mistress of the house was visiting her ailing aunt in Austria, that esteemed lady's home country. The call of the master at that time of night could mean only one thing. An icy fist of fear constricted her heart. Her feet felt suddenly leaden, unwilling to move at the command of her panicked, desperate mind.

"Gyorgyike! Did you hear me, stupid girl?"

The door to her tiny, bare, and drafty room was flung open, almost ripping it off the hinges. The sound of the master's drunken voice singing an old Hungarian folk song filtered up the stairwell from his quarters. Gabor, Gyorgyike's little boy of barely three years old, ran to her and hid himself under her skirts.

The plump, scowling housekeeper, her double chin wobbling irritably as she shook her head, marched into the room, her skirts rustling busily. "Get yourself out there, girl, before he flares into a temper," the woman commanded, reaching in under her skirts and dragging out a mute, terrified Gabor. "You know he doesn't like to be kept waiting when he calls on us."

Gyorgyike found her own temper flaring as the housekeeper roughly shoved her son into a corner of the room, and he scrambled under the bed, but she bit her tongue. "I'm sorry, I'll go right away," she said, bobbing her head submissively. She knew quick action would appease the housekeeper and the couple of floors down to the master's chamber would give her time to think of something, some alibi she could use to escape the man's dreaded attentions.

But when she stepped into the plush, ornately decorated room, so vastly different from her own, her mind was still a dark, foaming ocean of fear, with not a single idea bobbing to the surface. Trying not to retch, she allowed herself to be drawn roughly into the master's groping, grasping embrace.

Turning her face away to avoid the worst of the alcohol on his breath, she went to the safe place in her mind, wishing she could be dead, but knowing she could never end her life now that she had Gabor. He was the only good thing that had happened to her since her parents had died and they had taken her on as a kitchen maid at the tender age of twelve years.

The abuse had started soon after her fifteenth birthday, when some of the other servants had despised her for her natural beauty. A beauty she wished she didn't have since it had cost her all her innocence, something far more precious to her than the admiration of people who knew nothing of her inner hell.

The master paused in his pawing and sniffed at her décolletage. "What is that smell?" he asked, wrinkling up his nose like a spoiled child.

Gyorgyike snapped back to the present moment, remembering she had been helping to preserve onions that whole day and had not yet washed up when the housekeeper called her to the master's quarters. "It's onions, my lord," she said simply. "I did not have time to bathe before…"

He shoved her away in disgust before she could finish her sentence. "You'll make me gag!" he yelled. "Go get yourself cleaned up, you hussy! Come to me stinking like a street whore! How dare you?"

Gyorgyike ducked, anticipating the blow that came whizzing past her left ear, and scurried from the room. Her chest was a whirlwind of emotions. Fear ruled the roost, as always, but just beneath, a slowly growing glow of hope flickered, fueled by a frantic desire to escape what she knew would happen next.

Once he was in a temper, the master rarely became docile again, and the molestation would turn to abuse, leaving her with the black and blue marks of his wrath for weeks to follow. Even if she came back clean and smelling of lavender and roses, he would exact his ire for daring to insult him to begin with.

This time, however that she had a window of opportunity was not lost on her. Dashing up to her room, she coaxed Gabor out from under the bed. "Come with me, my kicsim," she choked, urging him along. "Nobody is going to hurt us ever again."

Gabor looked up at her, his eyes wide black pools of terror and yet trusting her implicitly as she struggled into her coat. Now that she needed to get away in a hurry, the insubordinate sleeves seemed to resist her arms of their own accord. At last, mother and son were bundled up warmly, and she ushered her son toward the door of their room.

Checking the corridor to make sure the housekeeper wasn't in sight, she hurried down the back stairwell that only the servants used, her heart pounding in her throat. She paused at the bottom of the stairs, peering into the moonlit courtyard. All was quiet. Only the chirping of crickets and they could hear the occasional snorting of a horse.

As they ducked across the courtyard and into the stables, she heard the master's voice yelling her name. He was hardly giving her time to get cleaned up. Scaling the ladder into the loft, she made a space among the hay bales where they could hide and not be seen. Hunkering down, she held little Gabor in her lap while chaos developed all around them.

The master was irate, yelling at the housekeeper and everyone else to find the kitchen girl and find her fast. Servants went rushing around, calling her name. A couple came into the stables, one of them climbing up into the loft. Gyorgyike held her breath. She could see the light from the lantern flitting across the roof above her as she pressed her son's head against her chest.

She knew he would not make a sound. Not a peep had come out of him since he had grown old enough to understand the meaning of the sights and sounds around him. The housekeeper called him deaf and dumb, but more often, she called him stupid. Gyorgyike knew that was not true. Gabor's dark, perceptive eyes spoke to her more deeply than any words she could remember an adult speaking after her parents' deaths.

At last, the furor died down, the search was abandoned, and the master's raucous, drunken singing and cursing eventually died down as the effects of the copious drafts of alcohol he consumed took their full toll. Gyorgyike waited a little longer, in case the housekeeper had got it into her head to lie in wait for her. The woman was heartless, but she was sharp as a whip.

Gyorgyike didn't know how long she had nodded off, but she woke to Gabor tugging at her sleeve. Starting awake, she looked around her frantically, for a moment not remembering why she was up in the stable loft. Then clarity hit her, and she stood up, peering down at the nearest window. It was still pitch dark outside.

Hoisting her son up onto her hip, Gyorgyike made her way down the ladder, stopping every couple of steps to listen for any sound that might give away the approach of the housekeeper or another servant, but the homestead was silent. Even the crickets seemed to have gone to sleep.

A quick forage in the kitchen armed her with a loaf of bread, a hunk of cheese, and a flask of water. Without a backward glance over her shoulder, Gyorgyike headed for the road. If she had slept long, she would not have much time before it was light, and the city of Budapest was a good two hours' walk away. She knew because she had tried to run away before—unsuccessfully.

Half running, half walking, her heart pounding in her throat, she kept to the bushes on the side of the road, hoping against hope that nobody would see her and take advantage of her. Gabor scurried along behind her, raising little more protest than breathless grunts of effort at her frantic pace across the muddy earth, after which she would hoist him up on her hip to give his stubby legs a chance to rest.

At last they reached the city, shadowy and brooding beneath the light of a waning gibbous moon. There was a soup kitchen she knew of near the Danube River. If she could just get in there somehow for a few days until she figured out what to do next, at least she and Gabor would be fed.

Sneaking into the alley beside the soup kitchen, she found an empty wooden crate and crawled inside it, taking Gabor with her. They huddled together against the cold, thankful to be hidden from sight. Gyorgyike dozed fitfully, her senses alert to every sound and scent around her until the first glimmer of dawn filtered through the slats of the crate.

Blinking, she rubbed her eyes and peered outside. A newspaper lay discarded on the cobblestones in front of her face. It was open to the classified pages. A bold heading in ornate letters printed in black on the paper caught her eye: "A New Life Waits in the New World! Mail-Order Brides Needed in America!"

For a moment, everything around her faded. Only the black letters on the ivory paper existed. A new life? Was it a sign? This was just what she needed. A new life away from the hell she had been living since her twelfth birthday. On the one hand, being a mail-order bride meant she would have to allow the attentions of a man again. But if it was a man looking for a bride, at least she had the chance of being treated like a lady instead of an unwilling woman of the night.

She had heard the New World was a vast open space with many unexplored places. If she didn't like her new husband, she could simply leave him and make a life for herself and Gabor some other way. There were even whisperings of women in the New World running their own homesteads without a husband.

It felt as if a door was opening at the end of a long, dark, cold tunnel. A dazzling, warm light was shining into her desperate world. Grabbing the paper, Gyorgyike tore off the advertisement. There was an address and the name of an agency. It wasn't far from the soup kitchen.

Her heart pounding in her chest, she grabbed Gabor's hand and emerged into the slowly wakening city. There were already merchants' delivery carts doing their daily rounds, the chimney sweeps with their grubby clothes and equally grubby faces going from door to door, the milk wagon hurriedly finishing the last of its rounds before the streets burst into full, busy life.

Gyorgyike could almost smell the fresh air of an untainted countryside, feel the sun on her face and the wind in her hair, imagine the wide-open unwalled space all around her, drink in the freedom of deciding for herself where she would go and when she would go there. It was intoxicating and energizing, drawing her like a moth to a flame. She hardly thought of the possibility that she might get burned.

***

Connor Slade slicked back his wavy black hair and stroked down his mustache, twirling the ends slightly as he perused his reflection in the makeshift mirror of the train station building. He did not consider himself an ugly man, with his aquiline nose and piercing blue eyes inherited from his English grandfather, though he would like to be a little taller and have broader shoulders. He straightened the black strings of his necktie and smoothed down his coat.

He looked around the station at the handful of other people waiting for the train from New York to arrive. There were some families, probably waiting for a grandparent or an elderly aunt. A few bored-looking men in bowler hats holding placards, ostensibly with names on them for the expected travelers, stood around as well. An old but sprightly lady peered down the track now and then, a slightly anxious expression on her face.

Suddenly, her eyes widened and, as they did, Connor heard the far-off, shrill blast of a train whistle. He followed the old lady's gaze to see the train chugging into view, smoke puffing from the stack. He sucked in his breath, smoothing his hair down again. The pictures of the woman he had arranged to meet here had already made his stomach flip-flop. He could hardly imagine how she might make him feel when he saw her in real life.

The train screeched into the station and came to a grinding, puffing halt. Connor swallowed, scanning the doors of the coaches. A porter stepped briskly forward and opened the door of the coach in front of him. He was not at all prepared for the vision that filled the doorway. She was every bit as beautiful as her picture, and more so.

Her face was oval with a strong, but not masculine, jawline. Two large, heavy-lidded, golden-brown eyes, festooned with thick black lashes, dominated the ivory skin of her face. Her nose was petite and slightly upturned, and her mouth curved gently above a rounded chin that gave her a cherub-like appearance. Rich, black curls framed her features, falling loose from a simple bun pinned up on the crown of her head.

"Gyorgyike Szarka?" Connor rasped, realizing too late that he had lost control of his voice. He coughed, repeating her name in a clearer tone while he dropped his eyes, unable to look into hers. What he noticed in this new perspective didn't help him. The plain gray dress she wore perfectly accentuated the gentle, womanly curves of her body, which he was happy to note was shorter in stature than his own.

"I am Gyorgyike Szarka. You are Connor Slade, yes?" Her voice came to him as if from another dimension entirely, but not merely because of her stunning beauty. As she stepped down from the train, a little head of tousled black curls, even tighter than hers, appeared behind her skirts. Two frightened black eyes stared out at Connor from a pale face.

Connor felt his stomach clench. She had not mentioned a child in any of her letters. Not a word. Not even a hint. He looked up into his mail-order bride's face. "There are two of you?" he asked abruptly, her beauty suddenly losing its effect on him.

She held his gaze, almost defying him to send her away. "I did not tell you of my son, Gabor, because I know you will not let me come if you know. But I cannot leave him there in Hungary."

Connor took a deep breath. Though she spoke with a thick accent, he understood her meaning. He hadn't prepared himself for a stepson, and it irked him she had lied about something that significant. What else might she be hiding from him? A moment of tension hovered between them.

Gyorgyike remained defiant and proud, her chin held high while she continued to hold his gaze and her little boy peered at him from behind her skirts.

He couldn't very well toss them out on the streets. Especially after they had just traveled halfway across the world to reach him in Boston. The child seemed scared, but not like most children, who might simply be naturally wary of a stranger. There seemed to be a deeper fear, a fear not born of imagined future events but of experience. Connor let out the pent-up air in his lungs with a long sigh. "I'm not the kind to leave a woman and a child destitute," he said gruffly. "You have any bags that need carrying?"

Gyorgyike shook her head, looking slightly relieved at his response but still proudly holding her chin high. "We have nothing but the clothes on our backs," she responded.

Connor nodded. He had clearly picked a lemon, as beautiful as that lemon might be. Still, he had to hope that somehow, they could work things out. "I have to warn you," he said as he turned and led the way to his waiting horse and buggy. "I've made plans for us to join the Emigrant Road to Oregon, and it won't be a simple journey for a little child like yours."

Gyorgyike gave him a surprised look, her exquisitely shaped eyebrows arching in two perfect crescents above her heavenly eyes. "Oregon? I have heard of it. They say it is like paradise."

"Yeah, that's what they say," Connor replied grimly. "But there are the great American plains to cross before we reach it. You sure you and, uh, Gabor will make it?"

"We have already come this far. I think we can go to Oregon."

Connor couldn't help but notice a strange light in her eye, as if she expected the realization of a long-awaited dream. What was strange about it was that he got the distinct impression the dream didn't have as much to do with him as he had hoped it might.

# Chapter 2
# The Applegate Cutoff

Connor busied himself greasing the axles and making some last-ditch repairs to the creaking wooden wagon that had carried them across so many miles of prairie and mountain trails and clearly bearing the scars of that arduous journey. He smirked wryly to himself, considering how he had also not gotten off lightly from the rigors of the trail.

His usually strong frame had become quite gaunt, his cheekbones more prominent, and his shoulders even a little stooped, although he tried to remind himself often to square them. Not only had his body changed because of the terrain they had covered across the Great American Desert and the aptly named Rocky Mountains, but his heart had taken a beating, too.

His initial shock of finding out about Gabor's existence, as well as his subsequent dread of the responsibility of caring for the boy as a father would, had worn off quickly. Gabor had proven to be a withdrawn and quiet little fellow who never spoke a word. The fear in his eyes had slowly given way to trust as they traveled the trail, and Connor found himself quite attached to the boy.

In fact, the sentiment seemed to be mutual. Gabor would sometimes run up to Connor after his forays into the wilderness with his friend, Fiona, the little red-haired daughter of one of the other couples in the wagon train. Holding out a gift for Connor, he would look up into his face with his silent black eyes that spoke more than any words possibly could.

The little wooden box Connor had made to house all these gifts was full almost to the brim with bird feathers, dead insects, and even the discarded skin of a snake, along with other treasures and trinkets found along the trail.

Connor wished Gabor's mother could offer him gifts in the same way as her son. He sometimes took her a wildflower or a pretty bird's egg that he found, but her responses were always a curt nod of the head and a polite, "Thank you," with her large brown eyes averted from his face.

As the miles between them and Boston had stretched longer and longer, Connor had fallen deeper in love with his mail-order bride. But the emotional distance between them seemed to stretch at a pace, almost doubling that of the wagon train's progress across the unforgiving landscape. If only he could make her love him, but her heart was clearly a walled fortress.

He watched her emerge from the wagon, climbing out of the wagon box and onto the driver's seat in front before she hopped down by stepping on the front wheel.

"We are to get supplies for the rest of the trail, yes?" she asked blithely.

Connor wondered if she would have acted the same way if she had known about the thoughts running around in his head. "I suppose it's a good idea to start now," he replied, smiling at her. Her lips pursed a little, and she looked away.

"You know where Gabor is?" she flung over her shoulder without returning his smile as she stepped over the wagon tongue, apparently intent on making her way over to the supply depot within the plastered adobe walls of Fort Hall.

"He's over at the Tanners' wagon with Fiona," Connor informed her, the smile fading from his own face. He followed sadly in her wake, wondering what he could do to win her affections.

They had scarcely walked five paces from the circled wagons when two young men came striding toward them, animated with excitement as they discussed something. Matt Henderson and Brady Morland were the sons of the two men who had emerged as the leaders of the wagon train because Landon Morland was the most knowledgeable about the ways of the prairie and Clyde Henderson was a strong, dependable, honest man who will learn.

"Hey, Connor, Gyorgyike!" Brady cried out excitedly as he and Matt approached. "A feller just told us about another trail. Looks like it's a better choice than the old route, no rapids and fewer mountains!"

Connor had to admit, the prospect of the much-bespoken rapids of the Columbia River—known as the Dalles—and the Blue Mountains, with fall creeping steadily closer and temperatures seeming to drop by the day, was one that he was happy to avoid if he could. "Sounds like it's worth investigating," he responded, pausing as the young men reached them. "You told your pa about this yet?"

"On my way there," Brady assured him, moving to fulfill his mission.

Connor turned to Gyorgyike as Matt and Brady moved on, keen to share their newly gained knowledge with the rest of the settlers in their group. "Might be a good idea to hold off on buying supplies till we know the details of this other route," he said.

Gyorgyike nodded silently, and they followed in the two young men's wake. When they reached the circle of wagons once more, Brady and Matt were already sharing their find with a group of listeners made up of both their fathers and some of the other settlers.

"Instead of going up over the Blue Mountains to the Columbia and having to deal with the rapids, we can go down south a way, then straight across to the west, and up into the Willamette Valley from the south," Matt was explaining.

"Who told you about this?" Landon inquired skeptically.

"Some feller advertisin' what he calls the southern route," Brady volunteered. "Some folks are calling it Applegate's Cutoff. Seems like there's a lot of 'em headed out that way already."

"Well, I can't say I'll miss floatin' my ol' rickety wagon down a river full of rapids," Noel Tanner piped up, a grin spreading across his face. "The thing's fallin' apart as it is, without bein' thrown about like a cowboy breakin' a bronc."

"Hmmm..." Landon said thoughtfully. "I heard about the Applegate brothers. Some folks reckon they know their stuff, blazin' trails and all. Lost two of their boys to drowning in the

Columbia, that's why they were lookin' for another way around for the rest of the folks. Or so the stories go."

"You think we should try it, Mr. Morland?" Matt asked, his face looking eager. He apparently also liked the idea of skipping the rapids.

"Might be worth it," Landon said, nodding.

Connor felt his spirits lift. He had been dreading the rapids himself, as well as the chance of snow when they were crossing the Blue Mountains, but this looked like a way to avoid both. He shuddered at the thought of little Gabor being swept under a relentless, heartless river current.

"I've a feeling we'd be well advised to find out a bit more about it before we commit," Clyde Henderson said slowly, his eyes thoughtful. "I've learned, when a thing seems too good to be true, it usually is."

"We don't have a lot of time for investigations," Connor retorted, feeling a little irritable. "Winter's on the way, and we still have the Blue Mountains ahead of us."

"That's true," Clyde agreed patiently. "Thing I'm worried about is the route isn't well known. At least we'll know what to prepare for on the beaten track, thanks to all who went before us. Besides, it won't take more than a day or two to find out more about this Applegate Cutoff. That surely won't make a difference in the big scheme of things."

"I'm up for some adventure myself, heading off into unknown territory," Matt said hopefully, his eyes clearly willing his father to give up and go along with the consensus that seemed to form around the matter.

Clyde gave his son a fatherly smile. "I'm sure you are, Matt. My old bones just don't have it in them anymore. I heard tell there's a new cutoff up near the Dalles, too. They call it the Barlow Road."

"I heard of that one," Noel chipped in. "That Barlow feller who started it, he's got toll gates up. Askin' folks five dollars a wagon, plus a dollar for each head of livestock."

A collective gasp went up.

"And he's got five of them gates along the route to Oregon City," Noel added gravely.

Connor focused his gaze on Landon. The man was usually the one who made the final decisions around the camp, even though everyone was well aware he consulted with all the menfolk before he did so, when time and circumstances allowed. The little group of emigrants trusted his judgment, and not without reason. There had been many times along the trail when Landon's cool head and shrewd assessment of a situation had saved their skins.

"What do you think, Landon?" Connor said. "Is it worth risking the wagons and the livestock on the old trail up to the Columbia River or paying through our noses when we have an alternative? Surely those fellers won't be advertising their trail if they're not sure it's a better option."

Landon contemplated him thoughtfully for a while. "I've learned t' heed ol' Clyde's gut feelin' about a thing," he said at length. "He's right about one thing for sure, I'll own. A day or two won't set us back enough to make much of a difference in the conditions on the trail if we choose to go up to the Columbia."

Matt and Brady looked disappointed. Connor felt frustrated.

Noel Tanner held up a hand. "I'll do some askin' around," he said briskly.

Connor did his best to shove aside his irritation. If he had learned anything on the trail, it was that dissent in the group was a dangerous thing.

The group who had split off from them to take the Sublette Cutoff near Fort Bridger had not made it across the barren wastes. The last the remaining emigrants had heard, only three of the men had come out on the other side with a single wagon, their party decimated by fatigue, hunger, and thirst, their wives, and children, the hapless casualties.

Connor shuddered at the memory. "I'll do a bit of digging myself, too," he volunteered.

Landon gave him an impassive look, but Connor caught the glint of gratitude in the leader's eye. The more people were asking around, the sooner they could make a more informed decision.

One task that needed to be performed, regardless of which route they chose, was to have their remaining ox's shoes checked and replaced if necessary. Connor was ever so grateful he traded off his mule for an ox a ways back. Connor led the patient beast over to the fort, where an enterprising ironsmith had set up shop nearby. It was a crude affair, but it got the job done, and the man made a living. Or so Connor assumed.

"The Applegate Cutoff?" the ironsmith echoed in response to Connor's question, his face darkening as he spoke.

"Yeah, that's the one," Connor confirmed. "I was wondering if you knew anything about it." He guessed someone who had been around the fort a while might have picked up on some news, especially someone who offered such a necessary service for travelers with ox wagons.

"Oh, I know the Applegate Cutoff all right," the man spat. "Worst decision I ever made."

Connor snapped to attention. Those were not the words he had expected. "The way I heard it, it's a way for families to avoid dying in the rapids."

"Well why don't you mosey on out there and save yer skins?" the smith replied caustically. "Though I can't say you'll find the Paiutes less of a worry than the Dalles, if you were askin' my honest opinion." He lifted the ox's hoof and peered at the worn leather shoes on the animal's cleats. Removing them with a grunt, he measured the old shoes against some already made iron ones hanging from a wire hook.

"Nobody said anything about Paiutes," Connor said hesitantly, aware the smith wasn't just looking for an ax to grind. His eyes testified to untold pain and regret rather than anger or bitterness.

"Sure, they didn't. If you were sellin' omelets from eggs you already paid for, would ya be tellin' folks about the shells in 'em?"

Connor found it an interesting metaphor, but the meaning was not lost on him at all. "You or someone you know get some of those eggshells between their teeth?" he asked, feeling genuinely sympathetic.

"You could say so," the smith replied between hammering the nails of the new shoe into the ox's hoof. He avoided Connor's eyes as he spoke, focusing on the job at hand. "It was me and my wife, and our two chickabiddies. My younger sister came with us, too. Scarce eighteen she was, and sweet on a wholesome young feller in the wagon train. Good manners. Knew his place."

Connor nodded but didn't reply. The man's words made him aware that was not the end of the story.

"Paiutes didn't like us cuttin' through their lands. Afterward, we heard some young no-accounts from a previous wagon train raided their camp and stole some horses. Killed the Paiutes who tried t' stop 'em. After that, I reckon they figured they'd strike first. Them Paiutes don't take chances protecting their own. Anyhow, they attacked, and now it's just me left of my family. Wagon burned and everythin' in it. Nothin' for me t' do but hang around here and see where the winds blow me next."

Connor's heart constricted in sympathy. The man's voice was unemotional, but Connor knew it camouflaged a mountain of pain and regret. "I'm truly sorry for your loss, sir," Connor whispered.

The smith grunted. "Don't let 'em tell you there ain't mountains, either. Family I heard of got stuck in three feet of snow, only the papa got out still suckin' air, and he went plumb loco after losin' his family. The original fellers who started that trail they meant well, an' they helped a few folks, I reckon. But the truth is there ain't a way a body's goin' t' get off lightly if he wants t' make it to the promised land. Manifest destiny and all..." He broke off to spit in the dirt as he lifted another hoof. "There's a price t' pay for it, no matter which route you take. We're all goin' t' see the elephant some time or another. Just gotta count the cost an' cut your losses, as my ol' pappy used t' say."

Connor sat quietly while the smith completed the job he had been given. The man's words had sobered him. A slow regret was building for the way he had resisted Clyde Henderson's call for deeper investigation. He was hasty in setting up his homestead, but he had to admit that getting his wife and stepson there alive was a necessary ingredient in his quest for the fulfilment of his own personal destiny.

In his mind, he had reasoned that perhaps Gyorgyike's reticence and withdrawal from him was at least partly because of the harsh conditions she had to endure on the trail. After all, he hadn't even warned her she would accompany him across an entire, vast continent after she had already traveled halfway around the world to become his bride.

Perhaps if he could get her settled, give her a home with some of the creature comforts that were so glaringly lacking in a life lived in a jolting, creaking wagon, exposed to the elements and a glut of known and unknown dangers, she might warm up to him and allow him close.

That afternoon, around the communal campfire of the four-family alliance, the men shared the information they had gleaned during the morning. Everyone listened intently while Connor told his story, and when he was done, the silence hung around the group a little longer.

"Fits what I heard, too," Noel piped up after a while. "There're mountains on the southern trail, too. And the route is longer, plus it cuts through the top edge of the desert. There ain't a river for miles."

"I heard it's fallen into disuse mostly in the last two years," Clyde added. "There are few families that go that way anymore. Most of them end up turning back."

"I guess we wanted an easy way round, but it's looking like that doesn't exist out here," Matt interjected thoughtfully, his voice sad.

"Ain't any shame in that, sonny," Landon reassured him gruffly. "We're all plumb tuckered out and stretched to our limits. Thanks to your pa, we've just been saved a bunch of trouble."

Matt nodded, looking over at his father. Connor couldn't help noticing the glow of something akin to hero worship in the eighteen-year-old boy's eyes. He wondered if Gabor would ever look at him that way, and the thought surprised him, but not for long. It would be a proud moment to see a young man looking up to him as a role model and a hero. But that had no chance of happening if he could not get the boy's mother to stay with him.

As they spent the afternoon preparing for the trail ahead, Connor kept a furtive watch on his wife. Although her dresses were stained and worn and hung on her far more loosely than they had when she had stepped off the train in Boston, she seemed to Connor to have become more beautiful as the weeks on the trail had passed.

The guarded sullenness was almost gone, and he often caught her reveling in the wilderness's beauty around them. But whenever he spoke to her or tried to share in her moments of wonder, a veil seemed to fall over her eyes, cutting him off from her heart.

*You've got only a few more months, Connor,* he told himself. *Better step up your game or you might lose the woman you love.* Somehow, losing her to her own heartless indifference felt worse than anything else.

# Chapter 3
# Insanity

Gyorgyike gazed in wonder at the scene before her. It was more exquisite than anything she had yet seen along the trail from Independence. The great Danube River that flowed through Budapest had always held her captivated as a child, but there was something different about the river she was staring at now. It possessed a wildness that touched something in her spirit and made her yearn even more for the freedom that had evaded her for most of her life.

Her favorite outing with her parents since she had been big enough to walk had been to climb one hill beside the Danube and look out over the broad river and the sprawling urban bustle below. She had felt removed from the busyness and the crush of humanity, gulping in the clean air after the effort of scrambling up the last incline to the top.

She had always imagined herself as a bird, soaring way up high over the puffing chimney tops and reaching spires of the buildings below, detached from it all and yet somehow in harmony with the pulsing rhythm of the hordes of humanity below.

Now there was no city, only massive boulders and soaring cliffs. There were no chimneys and spires, only tall fir trees reaching up to the heavens, seeming to mimic the towering peaks in the distance that dwarfed anything manmade. A hawk called, wheeling above her in a sweeping, majestic arc. A sigh of longing caught in Gyorgyike's throat.

"Beautiful, isn't it?" Connor's voice said behind her, startling her slightly.

She had sneaked away from the nooning party, wanting to be alone for just a few moments. Irritation rose in her mind. If only he hadn't come to bother her, she could have hung onto the sweet peace for a few moments longer before the arduous journey resumed. She didn't respond to his question. It hardly needed a response, anyway.

For a few moments, they stood awkwardly side by side. Gyorgyike kept her arms folded and her eyes riveted on the scene before her. Connor fidgeted a little, shifting his weight from one foot to another. He had seemed to get more and more eager for her attention lately, and it was working on her nerves. She had not told him of her plans yet. It was too early. At least, that was what she told herself.

"Landon sent me to come get you," he said at last with a little cough. It felt as if he was apologizing for disturbing her moment of peace.

Gyorgyike reluctantly softened toward him. "We are ready to go so soon?" she asked, knowing full well the little band of only seven wagons, which had dwindled from an already small number of thirteen, never took long to stop for a lunch of crackers and dried meat and whatever might be left over from the night before—which usually wasn't much.

"Yeah," Connor responded, twiddling his thumbs. "Landon wants to make the river crossing up ahead before nightfall so we can start fresh in the morning without a lot of hard labor."

Gyorgyike wondered if Connor would ever do anything without Landon giving the order first. He seemed to always follow the leader. Gyorgyike secretly despised him for that. She was making her own decisions, forging her own path. It only proved to her she could not be caught up with a man who let others decide for him.

The insistent little voice that told her she was only looking for excuses not to be held down by any man at all drowned out with a response to Connor. "Well, then I suppose we had better go," she said, trying not to sound too sarcastic. The pained look on his face whenever she spoke harshly or drew back from his attention was as tiresome as the attention.

Connor nodded, and they both turned back to the campsite. On the way down the incline, she stumbled a little, and Connor reached out to support her, but she pulled her hand away and righted herself, stepping out and getting ahead of him so she didn't have to see the sadness in his eyes.

Despite the surrounding beauty, Gyorgyike knew it would deeply relieve her when they had finally made it to the Willamette Valley and didn't have to stay constantly on the move. Her body ached from the miles and miles of walking. Even as a kitchen maid, she could not remember spending so many grueling hours on her feet.

The trail wound down from the heights of the clifftop, finally leading to a crossing, one of many they had to ford across the river already. The landscape simply did not allow for the wagons to keep going along one side of the river as they had while crossing the prairie beside the stretched out, shallow, muddy waters of the North Platte.

The Snake River made up for that by providing some of the best water they had the fortune of drinking since the little oases of Alcove Spring and Ash Hollow early in their journey. Fresh and sparkling, the river tumbled over the rocks where the river narrowed between cliff walls and ran deep and clear where the Snake's waters had carved out a deeper bed among the rocks or meandered along a small plateau before its next descent into a cascade or a pool.

By the time the wagon train reached the crossing area, the sun was already behind the tall mountain crags, and a chill wind nipped at any exposed skin. Gyorgyike pulled on her coat and dressed her son in his little coat, too, before she hoisted him up onto the wagon. As she buttoned the garment, she noted it was getting a little small for him. And deserted clothing chests had become scarce along the trail. She sighed. Just a little longer.

The weary travelers stopped to splash the icy water on their faces, careful not to get their clothes too wet, although they knew their shoes and threadbare stockings would need to be dried by the fire as soon as possible after crossing over to the other side. With everyone refreshed, the crossing began.

One by one, they cajoled the weary oxen into the rushing waters. Landon and Noel, on their two sturdy mustang horses—as Gyorgyike had learned they were called— splashed in ahead of the first team, testing the footing in search of the most stable and hopefully also the shallowest way across. Men, women, and the older children helped with each crossing, pushing from behind or helping the wheels along.

This was the part that Gyorgyike enjoyed, and she knew Gabor enjoyed it, too. Her heart constricted a little as she thought of the possibility she might have to separate him from his friends and the little community that had become like an extended family to him. Especially his best friend, Fiona.

As she helped Anna carry some extra things across the river, holding the bundles high above their heads, she watched the two children enthusiastically petting the oxen who stood blowing on the opposite bank. Fiona was telling them in her resonant, clarion tones what good little oxen they were for working so hard and so obediently.

The creatures seemed to enjoy the ministrations of the children, but the adult humans were struggling. The bank onto which they rolled the wagons was higher than the one they had left and formed a little ridge the emigrants had to push the wagons over. To make matters worse, it was full of loose rocks they had to steady themselves on while heaving their heavy wood and iron-wheeled houses up out of the water.

Nobody even suggested clearing the rocks. Experience had taught them it was a fool's errand. Beneath the rocks would be slick, soggy earth or loose, sinking sand that proved even more difficult to get a wagon across. Stumbling and muttering and sweating, they completed their task, once, twice... until all seven wagons were safely across.

Gyorgyike felt close to tears. How many more crossings? How many more cold nights? How many more days of interminable walking? The knowledge she was not the only one thinking these things kept her from voicing her complaints out loud.

Silently, the emigrants set up camp. Words were not needed anymore. Everybody knew exactly what had to be done. They had been doing the same thing, following the same routine, night after night, for four months. Their movements were mechanical and slow. If Gyorgyike herself had not been so tired, she might have found it comical. As it was, the sight of them only added to her melancholy mood.

Only one camper still seemed to have a flicker of energy left in him. Young Billy Henderson, a spark of mischief still faintly visible in his eye, regaled the sleepy campers with a story he had heard told around the campfire of another wagon train stopped at Fort Hall at the same time as their own.

"Feller told a story about a lady called Elizabeth Markham," Billy said, his eyes glinting in the firelight that flickered across his face. The group of families huddled around the blaze, hoping to soak in as much warmth as they could to ward off the bitter cold that would assail them in the early hours before dawn.

"You listen to too many stories, Billy," his sister Tessie interjected. She was ten and had a practical mind. It showed most of all in the way she was always helping her carpenter father, Clyde, to repair wagons. Now it almost shut down Billy's attempts at entertaining the sluggish, phlegmatic pioneers.

"This ain't just a story. It's real," Billy insisted, growing more eager to tell it despite his sister's admonition. "Her husband was Samuel Markham, and they had five children. They called one of their sons John."

"Well, you'd better tell us about the Markhams, then, half-pint, or you won't get it out of your system," Landon said, a slight ripple of laughter just below the surface of his matter-of-fact statement.

Tessie sighed and threw a stick in the fire, but Gyorgyike listened with interest. The boy had proven to have a keen eye and a sharp mind. There wasn't much he didn't notice, and he seemed to remember details like few grown men could.

"Well, all right." Billy didn't need a second invitation. "The Markhams were traveling along this very Snake River, just like we are, and they were plumb wore out. Just like we are."

"Worn out," Tessie corrected him from beside her father.

"Plumb worn out just don't sound right," Billy retorted, unfazed.

"Doesn't sound right," Tessie held her ground.

"Hush now, Tess," Anna shushed her daughter. "Let Billy tell his story without you giving him a grammar lesson."

Tessie gave a little huff but obliged, crossing her arms over her chest and shifting closer to her mother for warmth.

"Well, Mrs. Markham, she got so she just couldn't face another day of walking, and one morning when the wagon train started out, she sat down by the side of the trail and refused to go a single step further." Billy looked around the group, waiting for someone to make a comment.

Noel nodded thoughtfully. "I reckon I've felt like doin' just that more than a few times already," he said gravely.

Billy smiled and continued, happy that someone was paying attention. "Well, of course, Mr. Markham wasn't too excited about that, and he got argumentative with her. They were slingin' words back and forth and eventually Mr. Markham said, 'If you ain't comin' along, well, you can just stay right here, then. See how much you like that.' And the rest of the wagon train went on, leavin' Mrs. Markham right there on the side of the trail, pouting." Billy paused again.

"That's a rather irresponsible thing to do," Helen Morland remarked disdainfully.

"Don't take this too much to heart, Helen, but you've threatened many times to stay behind on the trail," her brother, Brady, reminded her.

"I wasn't talking about her refusing to go further," Helen replied, her chin held high. "I was talking about her husband and the others leaving her there alone."

"Oh, that's not the end of the tale," Billy said, a gleeful glint coming into his eye.

Gyorgyike had to smile wryly at herself. The boy had found a juicy story, and he had evidently been rehearsing it in his head for the whole two weeks they had spent on the trail since leaving Fort Hall.

"Mr. Markham hadn't gone much farther when he sent their son, John, to go see if his mother was all right and if she had come to her senses. It was hours later when Mrs. Markham came back alone without John." Billy paused once more.

"Had John gotten lost?" Lucy asked, her voice breathless with suspense. She was one of the youngest of the Morland children at twelve years old, and it was clear to Gyorgyike that Billy was smitten with her. He had the same look on his face Gyorgyike saw on Connor's face every time their eyes met.

"I'll bet Indians got him. Or wolves," Helen said, shuddering at her own thought and casting a fearful eye at the gathering darkness.

"Neither of the two," Billy announced almost triumphantly. "When Mr. Markham asked his wife what had happened to their son, she said she had beaten him with a rock for trying to force her to come back and she thought he might be dead."

A gasp rose from the folks around the fire.

"Oh, that's awful!" Carrie, the Morland's oldest daughter, exclaimed. "She must have been quite beside herself to go that far! Beating her own son with a rock?"

"You're not making this up, are you, Billy?" his father cautioned him.

"No, sir," Billy said, shaking his head emphatically. "That's just how the story was told. And it was a dragoon telling it, too. He said it was God's honest truth."

"Well, I think we'd better have Dearbhla sing us a song to calm our nerves after that one," Anna said, referring to Noel Tanner's wife, who was of Irish descent and could sing like a nightingale.

"But the story isn't finished yet," Billy protested, a grin spreading across his face.

"There's more?" Helen groaned, rolling her eyes.

"I want to know if John really was dead," Lucy said, and Billy's chest puffed out. He had the attention of the object of his affection.

Gyorgyike saw Connor smile as Billy enthusiastically resumed his story, his focus now wholly on Lucy's mesmerized features.

"Mr. Markham and two other men hurried back to the place where they'd left Mrs. Markham, and there they found John, groaning in pain and half dazed but still alive," he recounted dramatically. "I'm sure you can imagine Mr. Markham was over the moon to find his son alive, but when he got back to the rest of the wagon train with his wounded son, he found his wife had set fire to their wagon."

Another gasp rose from the listeners, and Billy's face positively glowed. Without waiting for any further commentary, he finished his story with a flourish.

"Thankfully, some of the other pioneers put it out, and the Markhams reached Willamette Valley. I reckon they've got a homestead there now, and Mrs. Markham doesn't hardly set foot outside of her farmyard."

"Any way we can find out the Markhams' address?" Connor interjected, as Billy's audience devolved into a hum of muttered comments. "I think I'd like to make sure I set up my homestead very far away from theirs."

Billy erupted into peals of appreciative laughter. Noel, Brady, and Matt joined in, and soon the somber mood was broken.

"Well, the fire's almost embers, and I'm ready for a good night's shuteye," Landon cued bedtime for his family and their fellow travelers.

They met his announcement with murmurs of agreement all round, and soon Gyorgyike found herself inside the wagon, spooning with Gabor on their lumpy bed of boxes covered by a thin horsehair mattress.

Connor clambered inside and lay down behind her.

She stiffened.

"Mighty cold outside tonight," he muttered by explanation. They had agreed he would sleep under the wagon while she and Gabor slept inside. The closer they had come to Oregon, the colder the nights had become, and Connor had, to Gyorgyike's surprise, continued to sacrifice the relative warmth of the wagon for the sake of his wife's desire to sleep alone.

This was the first time he had broken that unspoken agreement, and she knew she couldn't really expect that of him anymore. There was a genuine chance he could die exposed to that kind of cold, and he didn't deserve that. Not after how patient he had been with her since she had set foot in Boston, as well as all along the trail.

She had almost wished he would get frustrated and give up on her, chase her and Gabor away. At least then she would be free. And yet a small seed of gratitude toward him was germinating in her heart. It would not be easy to leave him, but she knew she could not love any man. Not after what she had suffered at the hands of men in her life.

"That is all right," she said in a stilted monotone. At least if they lay together, they could keep each other warm. She felt herself slightly relax.

Connor grunted his thanks. Moments later, he moved closer. Gyorgyike stiffened again, her heart pounding fearfully in her throat. He placed his arm across her waist, encircling her and her son.

Gyorgyike felt a shock run through her, and she sat up abruptly. "That is too close," she stated flatly, staring into the darkness ahead of her as Connor's arm fell away.

"Just wanted us to all keep warm," Connor replied gruffly.

"I just wanted to…" Gyorgyike began, but quickly bit her tongue. Instead of echoing in the night air, the words she had choked back just in time rang in her head.

*I just wanted to marry you so I can make a life for myself and Gabor in the New World. I never really was your wife, and I never really will be.*

# Chapter 4
# Gate of Death

The Slades spent a fitful night, but Gyorgyike was secretly glad for Connor's extra warmth. He had kept his arms to himself for the rest of the night, but his presence behind her had comforted her, in some strange way. She began to reluctantly trust him. Although her guard was never fully down among any of the menfolk.

Too often she had seen the most outwardly respectable men turn into ravaging despots when they were out of the public eye and free to indulge their lewd secret passions. Her master in Hungary had felt himself obliged to offer her services to any of his guests who might take a fancy to her when they overnighted at the manor. And those guests had included dignitaries and esteemed gentlemen of the upper crust of society.

She even feared what might happen once she and Connor had their own little home in the valley, too far away from the others for them to hear her begging to be left alone. There were nights she woke up in a cold sweat from nightmares. Now that Connor was sharing the wagon with her and Gabor, she hoped she would never wake him with her thrashing about or calling out in her sleep and start him asking questions.

She pushed the dark thoughts aside, rising quickly at the sound of the morning wake-up call. The emigrants had dispensed with the rifle shot to wake the camp since they were few enough to be wakened by a simple vocal call or a spoon banging against a pan as some of the younger men liked to do at the end of their nightly vigil, Connor included.

This morning it was Clyde, patiently walking around inside of the circle of wagons and calling each family by name.

Gyorgyike thanked him as he passed by their wagon. "This is such a hard thing that you and the other men are doing," she remarked. "Losing a night of sleep even once a week, it will make a person too tired, no?"

"It sure does, Mrs. Slade," Clyde affirmed. "It helps, though, that we share a night between two men. That way, at least we only ever stand guard half the night."

"This is a good plan," Gyorgyike commented.

"It was Connor's idea that we keep on doing that, really, and sometimes he lets me sleep instead of waking me when it's my turn to stand guard the second half of the night," Clyde informed her. "You've got yourself a mighty good man there, Mrs. Slade. I've heard of mail-order brides who weren't so lucky as you. It's a gamble, but yours surely paid off."

Gyorgyike felt more than saw Connor emerge from the wagon and come to stand beside her. "You've got a brood of four, Clyde," he said, rubbing the sleep out of his eyes. "You need the sleep more than I do sometimes."

Clyde laughed his deep, throaty laugh and moved on.

Gyorgyike didn't know where to look. It was becoming more and more difficult to justify her plans to leave Connor, and yet she knew she could not bring herself to do anything else. She would not be a good wife to him. She would never let him close, not because he was a bad man, but because she could never let any man close.

For a fleeting moment, she wished things could have been different, but as soon as that moment had passed, she steeled her resolve. Wishes were for weaklings, people who expected life to make them happy, people who took happiness for granted, as if they believed they had a right to it somehow. She knew it was a privilege reserved for those who fought tooth and nail to create it in their own lives.

Without looking at Connor, she turned away to take care of the morning's chores. It would be better not to let herself get attached. Not to feel gratitude or admiration or affection of any kind for the man who thought he was her husband. That would be a kindness, not a cruelty, as most might assume.

Cruelty would be to make him think she loved him, only to break his heart in a far more devastating way. He would understand one day. More than that, he would thank her. She was sure of it.

Her conscience mollified, Gyorgyike focused on the day's travel. It was a task that took all her attention and determination. Her feet still hurt, and her body ached. The food they had was not enough to fill her belly and provide her with the energy she needed, but it was all they had.

Game was scarce here in the mountains, as were the berries and ground tubers that had been so prevalent on the plains. They had to ration what they had. It would be better to feel a little hunger now than to find themselves a week out from the next supply station without a bite to eat.

"We're going to camp at the Gate of Death," Gyorgyike heard Billy excitedly inform Lucy.

They trotted past her as she plodded along beside their two emaciated oxen that were straining against the yoke. Even Billy had been reduced from skipping everywhere he went to moving around at an almost sedate trot.

"The Gate of Death?" Lucy echoed, her tone of voice mirroring Gyorgyike's feelings of aversion to spending the night at a place with such a name.

"Oh, it's not really dangerous there," Billy assured her blithely. "It's just rumors, you know. Old wives' tales. There are folks who say the valley between the mountains is the perfect place for travelers to be attacked by the Shoshone who live around there. It's their territory we're in now, did you know that?"

Lucy shook her head to show she hadn't known that until that moment. "But what if they really attack one day?" the little girl asked earnestly. "What if they attack for the first time while we're there?"

The children moved out of Gyorgyike's earshot, and she couldn't hear Billy's response. She wouldn't have, anyway, since her mind was consumed with what he had said before that. It seemed a little foolish to overnight in a place so named.

She could understand the logic of seeking shelter from the frigid winds at night and the increasingly frequent rains that fell as winter steadily approached. But even the rumor of attack felt to her to be enough of a warning sign to stay away.

Her mind wandered back to snippets of stories she had heard men sharing in hushed voices when they thought there wasn't a woman listening. She knew little about the native inhabitants of the land, apart from the few who had mock-attacked the wagon train she was traveling with and the few who had helped them in troubled times.

What she knew was when men told stories out of female earshot, those were usually the true ones, and they had turned her blood to ice.

The name of their campsite that evening didn't seem to bother anyone else as much as it did her, though, and when evening fell, the four families and the other three wagons drew into a tight circle. The diminished herd of livestock grazed contentedly in the middle, while two large campfires warded off the darkness and the cold of approaching night.

Around those fires sat the families, sharing a meal and telling stories. Clyde Henderson played his fiddle while Connor accompanied him on his banjo, which was already down to four strings instead of the original five. Dearbhla, little Fiona's mother, sang a lilting Irish dirge that Gyorgyike could not understand, but she didn't mind. Her thoughts were consumed with the colossal bulk of earth and rock that towered over the campsite.

Now and then she threw a glance at the jagged black outline silhouetted against the pale orange sunset sky, watching for changes in that outline. She imagined figures rising over the top and raining down fiery arrows upon the helpless campers.

When the women were washing up after the evening meal, Anna looked at her in the dim lamplight. "You seem a little wound up, Gyorgyike," she said in her gentle, kind voice. "Is there anything the matter? Anything we can help you with?"

Gyorgyike felt startled at the question. She had always assumed she kept her emotions hidden well, even when she lived and worked in the Hungarian mansion. Now she wondered if the people she had lived among then had simply elected to ignore her inner turmoil and suffering. Or perhaps they had not even noticed it simply because they didn't care to take notice.

"Help me with?" she echoed, casting around for something to say to throw Anna off the scent. She couldn't let anyone know what was brewing in her heart. "I don't think so, no. But thank you very much for asking." She smiled what she hoped was a hopeful smile.

"All right but I want you to know if there's ever anything troubling you you feel you can't handle yourself. You're more than welcome to talk to me. I'd be happy to do whatever I can to help, and I know Clyde would say the same thing."

Gyorgyike nodded. "Yes, thank you," she repeated, feeling awkward and wishing Anna would leave her be, while wishing she could pour out her heart to the kind woman.

With the washing up done, the emigrants head off to bed one by one until only the last few souls, desperate for the fading warmth of the fire, and the man on night watch duty, were left. Gyorgyike lay between Connor and Gabor, wide awake. She listened to Connor snoring softly and Gabor breathing deeply and rhythmically while she stared at the canvas stretched across the wooden frame of the wagon.

Her eyes drifted to the revolver in Connor's gun belt hanging from a nail hammered into the thickest wooden hoop of the frame. Thankfully he had agreed to her insistence he teach her to shoot, and she had become known among her fellow overlanders for her steady hand and almost perfect aim. She had never wished death on anyone, but she had prepared herself for the day she might need to pull the trigger.

Mentally, she reminded herself the time was coming when she would have to get her own weapon. She wondered if Connor would buy her a gun. If he didn't, she would have to find something to trade for one, since she had no money of her own.

Suddenly a sound pierced her consciousness. It was a deep, rhythmic throbbing that seemed to vibrate through everything, right down to her bones. Gyorgyike held her breath and listened. Neither Connor nor Gabor stirred as the throbbing went on, seeming to grow steadily louder and faster.

The wind turned, and suddenly the throbbing was accompanied by a chorus of voices raised in a discordant yet hauntingly harmonious chant. She knew that sound. She had heard it often at the forts where they had camped. Sometimes a tribe camped nearby their circle of wagons, and she had heard them at their song and dance.

This chant seemed to her wary ears to be more intense, more urgent than the ones she remembered from before.

Landon's reply to her question about why they might engage in such a practice echoed in her mind.

*They're celebratin' mostly, but they also do song and dance t' curry favor with somethin' they call the Great Spirit and the other spirits of the prairie or the mountains. Mostly it's for rain, or a successful hunt, or for the buffalo season. Also, for war. They do it t' work up their nerve is what I reckon, though different folks think different things about why they beat the drums and chant like that.*

Whatever their reason was, Gyorgyike decided she wasn't about to wait around and find out. Rising quietly from her bed, careful not to disturb Gabor and Connor, she pulled on her coat and buttoned it up, then she slipped the revolver quietly from Connor's gun belt and hid it in the coat's pocket. Moments later, she was standing outside the circle of wagons, the chilly wind teasing at her tousled hair.

The sound was louder outside of the wagon. She peered into the middle of the circle. Norman Hastings, one of the other emigrants, was on watch. He sat by the embers of the fire, wrapped in a blanket, and trying to keep warm. He either hadn't heard the drums and chanting, or he thought nothing of it. Gyorgyike turned and began walking as quietly as she could away from the circled wagons toward the terrifying sound.

What was calling her to face her fears head-on, she didn't know. All she knew was that living with her nerves on edge, constantly expecting something to happen, was eating her up from the inside and compelled her to make something happen instead. At least that way she would have control.

Thankfully Norman didn't notice her departure, and after a while, she stopped worrying about how much noise she was making. The sound of the drums and the chanting were drowning out anything else, anyway. She quickened her steps almost to a run; conscious the sound was coming from behind the cliff face before her.

The jagged pillars of rock reaching up to the heavens seemed to vibrate with the sound, ominous and terrifying in the darkness. Driven by her determination to face her fear, Gyorgyike ran onward, around the rocks, and straight toward the huddle of cone-shaped lodges around a great bonfire blazing in the middle.

Her heart pounded in time with the drums being beaten by a group of men seated around them, all keeping the same rhythm while their voices rose and fell with their chanting, which grew more frenzied and shriller by the minute. The sound fed the fear in Gyorgyike's heart until she felt herself shaking uncontrollably, but still she advanced toward the campsite.

There were men and women in many brightly colored beaded and feathered accessories, including feathered headdresses and beaded tassels on their sleeves and trouser legs. Anklets made of what looked like shells and small bones acted like small percussion instruments as they danced around the fire, stomping their feet, and waving their arms up and down while they joined in the chant.

As she rushed headlong into the fray, a cry rose with a ripple of gasps. Gyorgyike planted her feet on the ground and pulled the revolver from her coat pocket, pointing it straight up at the star-studded sky. The drums faltered and stopped. The drummers standing to their feet and speaking to each other in their own language, clearly trying to make sense of what was happening.

"I dare you, any of you, to try hurt me and I will kill you wit' this weapon! I will kill you!" Gyorgyike screamed, waving the gun in the air. She kept turning around, conscious there were people on all sides and not wanting her back to any of them.

A young man with a hard, proud face pulled an arrow from a quiver behind his back and took aim at her.

Gyorgyike brought her arm down, her eyes focused on the young man's forehead. Her body felt hot and full of pins and needles. For a moment, her hand trembled.

Suddenly a woman's voice called out something in the tribe's language and a hush fell, replacing the confused murmurs of the villagers. Then the voice spoke in broken English. "We not hurt you," it said in a clear, ringing tone.

Gyorgyike looked around, trying to pinpoint where it was coming from.

"You not hurt us. We happy for hunting good. We have feast. You join us."

At last, the source of the voice stepped out from the crowd and into the space that had miraculously opened up around Gyorgyike. She blinked, trying to make sense of what she saw. The woman had long red hair braided into two pigtails, one hanging over each shoulder. Her skin was far paler than the others around her, although she was dressed just as they were. Her face was kind, and she smiled as she held out her hand.

"We not hurt you," she repeated, stepping slowly toward Gyorgyike.

"You are a white woman?" Gyorgyike asked, feeling distracted and disoriented.

"Yes, white woman in skin," the woman replied, smiling and nodding. "Shoshone in heart," she added, patting her chest with one hand. "I have Shoshone husband, live here long time. Since ten years."

Gyorgyike realized she had lowered the gun, which now hung loosely from her limp fingers. The murmuring had resumed, but it rang more of curiosity now than of worry and confusion.

"They did not hurt you, these savages? You live here wit' them?" she asked.

The woman waved one hand at the people gathered around and slowly moving closer as their curiosity overtook their fright. "No savages, just people. My people," she said, her green eyes full of tender affection.

Gyorgyike felt something inside her crumble. She dropped the gun into her pocket, covered her face with her hands, and sobbed. The earthy scent of leather and wood smoke filled her nostrils as gentle arms embraced and held her, rocking her slowly back and forth while a soothing voice hummed a strange but beautifully haunting melody in her ear.

# Chapter 5
# The Trappers

Connor woke in surprise to find the space between himself and Gabor empty. He sat up and peered around at the shadows under the wagon canvas. Gyorgyike was gone. The little boy was still sleeping peacefully, so Connor carefully removed himself from the wagon and looked around in the dim light of the moon to find his wife. Still, there was no sign of her. Worry began plucking at his heart.

Greg Sawyer, a bachelor who had been joined by Norman Hastings after his Aunt Mathilda Southey and her children had elected to follow the rebellious Marvin Peters along the Sublette Cutoff, was whittling something while he sat cross-legged beside a smoldering heap of coals that used to be a fire.

Connor stepped quickly closer. "Hey Greg," he said softly but urgently. "You seen Gyorgyike? She's not in the wagon anymore, and I can't see her in the camp."

Greg looked up, startled. "Gyorgyike? No, can't say I've seen anybody movin' about since I took over from Norman."

Connor felt his gut twist. "*He* mentioned nothing, did he?"

Greg shook his head. "Not a word," he replied, his voice also ringing with worry.

"I hate to wake him, but I have to know where she is," Connor said, moving in the wagon's direction the two bachelors shared. What he really wanted to do was wake the whole camp, but he knew that would be foolhardy to do. It would only invite chaos. Instead, he rapped on the wood of the wagon box and called Norman's name quietly.

A bleary-eyed, tousled head emerged from the opening in the canvas. "Connor? Wassamatter?" Norman slurred sleepily.

"You see Gyorgyike go anywhere while you were on watch?" Connor asked, keeping his enquiry as short and succinct as he could. His gut twisted into an even tighter knot at the sight of the young man shaking his head.

"No, saw nothing at all. Really quiet night," Norman replied. "Except for the powwow on the other side of the rocks."

Connor's blood froze in his veins. For the first time, he felt the cold biting his skin. "The powwow?" he repeated.

"Uh-huh," Norman confirmed. He pointed toward the jagged rocks that sheltered the camp. "Plenty of drummin' and chantin' goin' on last night. Reckon they had a good hunt yesterday."

"All right, thanks, Norman," Connor said, gesturing for the man to return to his sleep.

"Sure," Norman replied, and disappeared back behind the grubby canvas.

Connor walked back to where Greg sat, fanning the dying embers to life once more beneath a couple of fresh logs. "I'm going to look for Gyorgyike," Connor said to him. Greg looked up sharply, but Connor went on before he could get a word in. "Keep an eye on Gabor, will you? He's still sleeping in the wagon."

Greg nodded, apparently deciding it was better not to stop Connor. "Sure, I will. You sure you don't want t' take anyone with ya, though? We could wake some others…"

Connor held up a hand. "It's better if I go alone. Better they don't think it's an attack. If I need help, I'll come fetch some of you fellers. Thing is… I don't even know if I'm going to find her there."

Greg nodded, and Connor turned away.

He had traded his worn-out easterner boots for sturdy moccasins some Bannock tribe traders had been bartering near Fort Hall, and now he was grateful for them. The native people of this wild country sure knew how to walk softly, but he now learned they had at least some help from their footwear.

When the camp came into view beneath the pale moonlight, it was a peaceful scene. There were few people about, and no children. A few men sat around a fire, smoking a pipe they passed around from one to another. Periodically, one of them would cut a chunk of meat from a large joint roasting over the fire and chew on it slowly with a look of sheer ecstasy on their faces while they listened to their comrades speaking. Now and then, a ripple of laughter rose from the group.

Off to the side, Connor noticed some women in a little huddle of their own. As he watched, one of them stood up to hand something to another woman, and he saw with a shock it was his wife. For a moment, he froze, hunkered down behind the sagebrush that hid him from sight, and then he stood up and strode closer. It was clear she was there of her own volition. They did not seem to hold her by force at all. He wanted to know what was going on, why she had disappeared without a word in the middle of the night and left him to worry about her safety.

A muffled exclamation reached his ears from the direction of the group of men, but Connor kept walking. The women looked up from their chatter and stared in his direction.

"Gyorgyike," he said as he reached them and then stopped, suddenly feeling as if he were interfering in something he didn't understand. She stood up again and faced him, her features more peaceful than he had seen them for a long time.

"Don't hurt them," she said, her voice calm.

"Wasn't planning on it," Connor replied, feeling far less calm than his wife sounded. "What are you doing here?"

"The drums and chanting woke me. I came to see what was happening. Then I met this white woman who is the wife of the medicine man of this tribe."

Her words sounded like something out of a fairytale. Connor stayed stock still, staring at her, all the while vaguely aware of the jocular banter now being thrown around between the men. He realized he had clean forgotten to take his revolver from its hook in the wagon, and a horrible feeling of nakedness assailed him. "I was worried sick about you. Didn't know where you were or what had happened to you," Connor began, focusing on Gyorgyike instead.

"But now you see she is all right, yes?" another female voice reached his ears as a red-haired, clearly European woman dressed in traditional Shoshone dress stood up beside her.

Connor nodded, feeling unsure of what to do next. There was so much going on that completely contradicted the image of the Shoshone that he had been fed by most folks he had met ever since leaving Independence.

"Come, sit," the red-haired woman said, gesturing to him as she spoke. "You eat a little, then you go."

Connor decided, especially with the group of men sitting nearby, that it would be better to receive the woman's hospitality than refuse it and risk offending someone. He walked cautiously closer and sat down beside Gyorgyike.

He was handed a fragrant stew in what appeared to be a watertight basket, and he sipped at it slowly. It tasted blander than it smelled, but it was wholesome and filling, even warding off the nighttime chill. In silence, he listened to the women speaking. They seemed to ask Gyorgyike questions that the white woman, the medicine man's wife, would then translate for her.

They were asking about the white settlers, what they wanted in Shoshone territory, how long they would be there, what they ate, and various other topics. At last, when Connor's stew was consumed, and the women seemed to have run out of questions, Gyorgyike said, "Thank you for helping me. I wish you all well and I hope we can meet again one day."

"We hope also," the woman replied, smiling.

Gyorgyike rose and left the circle. Connor followed her lead, feeling as if he were walking in a dream.

"Gabor is alone?" she asked when they were out of earshot of their unlikely hosts.

"I asked Greg to keep an eye on the wagon for us. He was still sleeping when I went looking for you."

She nodded, and they walked on in silence for a while.

"You gave me a heck of a fright, Gyorgyike," Connor said, wanting her to know that what happened to her mattered to him.

"But everything is all right now, no?" Gyorgyike responded without looking at him.

"Sure, but could you just let me know next time?"

Gyorgyike stopped dead in her tracks. "There will not be a next time. This is one thing I must do alone. It is done, now."

In the morning, the campsite was abuzz with Gyorgyike's adventure. Greg and Norman pestered both her and Connor until Gyorgyike agreed to tell them what had happened. After that, the story spread like wildfire. Little Billy especially was enthralled and wanted to rush over to the Shoshone campsite himself, intent on making friends with the half-white children who lived there. His parents would hear none of it.

"Maybe one day I'll join a Shoshone tribe and marry one of their women," he said wistfully, staring out at the jagged rock outcrops that hid the magical campsite from his sight. "We'll live in a tipi and call our children names like Sings to the Moon or Roaring Bear."

"You better watch out or I'll start calling you Soft in the Head," Helen quipped caustically.

Billy threw a small rock at her that, thankfully, missed. Both children's parents called them to order, and then Anna spoke up.

"I think we'll all agree that Gyorgyike had a fine adventure, and I, for one, am grateful the good Lord kept her safe. Although I think perhaps we misjudge the intentions of the native dwellers of this land. So many of our kind think they are the savages but let us consider for a moment we are the ones trespassing on the lands they have lived on for generations—we don't even know how many." She smiled at Gyorgyike, who was smiling back with a sort of melancholy in her beautiful eyes. "Whatever Gyorgyike has learned about them and perhaps even herself, let the rest of us take it to heart."

Connor knew Anna's words were true, and he would have been happy to leave the story at that, but too many things bothered him. Why had she gone out to the camp in the first place? It was hardly likely they would have kidnapped her to let her walk free, especially since there was a white woman living among them as one of their own. What could have driven her to walk right into the enemy's camp if she had not known for sure what their reaction would be?

He had known since the day she had stepped down from the train in Boston with little Gabor peeking out from behind her skirts that she was a secretive and mysterious woman. In some ways, he had even found that attractive, but now it was weighing on him. What was she hiding? What dark secret of her past drove her to her strange and counterintuitive ways and reactions to things?

He could never know unless she told him. And that didn't seem to be something that was going to happen soon.

As the wagon train pulled out onto the trail that morning, rumbling away from the Gate of Death—which had turned out to be more a place of mystery than of terror—Connor rode out to the front with Landon.

"I'm feeling like I need some time to clear my head," he said to the wagon train leader as his horse drew abreast of Landon's. "If you like, I can go out and try a little hunting today. Maybe I can get us some fresh meat for supper tonight."

"I'm pretty sure nobody'll stop ya," Landon agreed. "Mind you take care now, though. We're gettin' into the mountains where the trappers are, an' they don't like folks competin' with them for their livelihood."

"Makes sense," Connor replied, nodding as he turned his horse's head away from the trail. He would keep the wagon train in sight as much as possible but ride out a little further from the trail where it was more likely he would find game. The rumbling, rattling approach of a wagon train could be heard far enough away to warn any wild animals from staying too long in the vicinity.

Striking out across the rocky, uneven terrain, he made his way between trees and rock outcrops covered with juniper and sagebrush. There was also rabbitbrush with its telltale fluffy, tufted seed balls that looked like rabbits' tails attached to the ends of their stalks.

Connor rode on, not paying as much attention to his surroundings as he had promised Landon he would. His head was still full of questions about Gyorgyike and her strange behavior. Racking his brains, he tried to remember anything she might have specifically said that would give him a clue to what she was hiding from him or what had driven her to approach a Shoshone camp in the middle of the night all by herself.

He kept drawing a blank, always coming back to the memory of how she had stayed far away from the camps around the various forts they had stopped at along the trail. She had always seemed to harbor an especially great fear for the native inhabitants of the Great American Desert, and yet he had found her in a huddle with their womenfolk, engaging in her own little powwow with them.

If not for the white woman with red hair who lived with the Shoshone, who knows what might have become of her, especially since she had been carrying a gun. His gun. He went cold at the thought as he remembered seeing her replace his weapon in the holster when she thought he was asleep. If she only knew he could not sleep a wink for the last few hours of that momentous night.

Perhaps that fact was also to blame for his lack of mental alertness, but he was jerked back to crystal clarity when a loud boom echoed against the black rocks scattered about, and a large mule deer burst from a cluster of juniper trees a few feet in front of him.

Without stopping to wonder where the boom had come from, Connor dug his heels into his horse's sides and sent the animal charging after the fleeing buck. There was a lot of meat on the animal. Enough to provide a hearty meal for the entire camp and extra meat for drying. Holding the reins in one hand and testing the utmost limits of his balancing skills, Connor drew his revolver and pointed it at the deer.

Waiting for just the right moment, when the animal was turned side-on as it negotiated a jumble of rocks, he pumped the trigger twice in quick succession, following the animal's trajectory. It gave a little leap into the air, landed on a rock, and tripped, crashing to the earth with a thud and a grunt in a cloud of dust. Attempting to rise, the animal stared at a rapidly approaching Connor and bawled as it struggled to regain its footing.

Connor took aim at the ribcage once more and fired another shot. The creature jerked and then collapsed, sprawled unceremoniously among the black igneous rocks. With his heart thumping wildly in his chest, Connor sprang from the saddle and quickly pulled out his knife. He slit the deer's throat and stayed kneeling beside his prize, wondering how he was going to get the large animal up behind the saddle all by himself.

He hadn't expected to come across anything this big. Maybe a couple of wild geese or some hares, but not a mule deer. He was still puzzling over what to do when his horse stomped and snorted. Connor looked up, knowing the animal always warned him when someone was nearby.

A bewhiskered, thickset man with piercing blue eyes and a beaver hat was approaching with a tall, gaunt-looking, redheaded fellow striding along behind him. They both had rifles slung over their shoulders, and the fellow behind looked a little irate. Connor felt outnumbered, but he stood up and acted nonchalant, hoping their intentions were friendlier than they looked.

"That is our buck," the first man said belligerently in a thick French accent, without so much as a "How do you do?" to Connor.

He hardly needed anything more than that to get his back up. "I don't see a name tag on him," he countered, "and since I just shot him, I'm not sure how you reasoned that out."

"It is very easy to reason out," the tall man spat in equally thick French-sounding tones. "Our shot missed because you scared off the buck with your crashing through the bush!"

"You're blaming me 'cause you missed your target?" Connor exclaimed incredulously, laughing in disbelief at the logic of the men.

"Oui!" the bigger man said, advancing closer, his hands balled into fists. "That is exactly what we are doing. Now, get out of the way, and we will take our buck."

"Just like a Frenchy to say that!" Connor snapped, pulling out his Colt and holding the barrel aimed level at the big man's chest.

The man stopped, his eyes flashing. His companion almost collided with him from behind.

"Just like all you varmints from Europe, matter of fact. You think you can just waltz in here and take what hardworking Americans broke their backs to build. Oregon belongs to us, and this dang buck belongs to me!"

The tall man fingered his rifle, his eyes looking shifty.

Connor pulled back the hammer on his gun with a loud click. Just at that moment, he had an idea. Help might have arrived after all. "Lay down your weapons and load that buck on the back of my horse. If you try anything smart, I'll give you a taste of my Colt."

# Chapter 6
# Trading

What he had expected Landon's response to be, Connor hadn't really considered, but when he led his buck-laden horse toward the circled wagons at nooning with two French trappers walking ahead of him at gunpoint, it was abundantly clear the wagon train leader wasn't impressed. He folded his arms, and his jaw began twitching the way it always did when Landon was exercising extreme self-control.

"Mind tellin' me what this is all about," he said, taking in the whole scene with one shrewd, sweeping glance.

"Your friend stole our buck and then 'e treated us like dirt," the large man said and spat on the ground to show his disgust.

"I didn't steal it, you were going to steal it from me," Connor countered hotly. He turned to face Landon. "It sprang out of the bush in front of me. I chased it down, and I shot it. It's mine."

"It sprang out the bush because you scare it away before we can get a good aim and shoot it," the tall man barked irately.

Landon focused his gaze on Connor's revolver that he still held pointed at the two trappers. "Holster that thing, cowboy," he said through gritted teeth.

Connor felt like a little boy again, being set straight by his father. "It was the only way I could think of to get the buck here without these two jumping me," he explained without being asked as he reluctantly slipped his gun back into the holster. Suddenly he realized how foolishly he had behaved.

"I'm sure we can reason this out like grown men," Landon said, his gaze roving over Connor and the two trappers.

"Yes, you can give us our buck and our guns, and we will leave you alone," the large man said, his belligerence toned down considerably under Landon's level stare.

Connor wished he could have that kind of effect on people, even though he knew it wasn't something that came easy. A man had to have lived through a whole lot of tough things to command the kind of respect Landon did.

"Now, that would be makin' it easy, but it wouldn't be makin' it fair," Landon replied in a tone that sounded like he was talking to himself as he folded his arms over his chest. "Seems to me all three of y'all had a hand in bringin' this ol' feller down, so I reckon it makes sense for y'all t' share it instead of fightin' over it like a cackle of coyotes squabblin' over a chicken carcass."

The tall man looked insulted, but he didn't say anything. The big man groused unintelligibly into his beard for a while, then he cleared his throat. "How were you thinking of sharing it?" he hedged.

"I reckon half and half would be reasonable. Since you fellers are only two, and my friend here was huntin' for a whole wagon train. You fellers are only two, ain't ya?" Landon spoke with deliberation.

"Oui, we are two," the large man admitted. He turned to his companion, and they deliberated in French for a few moments. Connor watched, wishing he knew what they were saying.

"All right," the large man said at last, turning to face Landon. "We will take 'alf the buck, but then we also take the skin."

"Sounds fair t' me," Landon agreed, shrugging. "Furs are your trade, after all, an' all we're lookin' for is our bellies filled." He paused and his eyes narrowed. "But I'm warnin' ya, if ya try t' pull off any of those things you suggested while you were parlayin' in French there, I'll be ready for ya."

The tall man went white and then red while he muttered under his breath to himself.

The large man's belly shook with silent laughter. "This young pup, 'e can learn something from an old dog like you, monsieur," he said wryly.

Connor knew he was the young pup being referred to, but he didn't say anything. He was wise enough to admit, to himself at least, that the Frenchman had a point.

Landon ushered Connor and the two trappers into the circle. The buck was hoisted down from the horse and butchered on the spot, the trappers taking the skin and wrapping their share in it. The large man lifted it up onto both their shoulders, and they marched from the camp looking quite comical with their lopsided burden.

Connor hastily wolfed down some hardtack, jerky, and a handful of dried fruit still left at the bottom of the barrel before the camp was broken up and the journey resumed.

"Connor, you'll ride up front with me," Landon instructed, and Connor knew there was no way he could even think of refusing the leader's order.

As the two men rode out ahead of the rest of the emigrants, Landon looked away to the horizon, scanning the hills and valleys, the rocky mesas and buttes with his hawklike eyes. Connor waited in silence for the lecture he knew was coming. He also knew he deserved it, so he prepared himself to listen rather than to try make some excuse or another where there wasn't any to be made.

"I reckon you don't have any idea what you almost brought on our camp, now, do ya?" Landon said at length.

"No, I don't," Connor admitted. "If I'm honest, I didn't think anything through at all. It all happened so suddenly, I just reacted from my gut, I guess."

"Well, sonny, you're goin' t' have t' learn t' react from your head next time. A man's gut is for digestin' food, a man's brain is for digestin' information. You got that?"

Connor nodded, doing his best to smother a smile. Landon had a way of saying things that always made even the most mundane statement sound profound. And he hit the nail on the head every time.

"Good. Now, just so we're on the same page, here, those Frenchies—as you call 'em—they were plannin' t' rob us later down the trail t' get back at ya for humiliatin' them. I would have made you apologize, but I figured your pride was already dented enough for me t' deal with ya. Better not t' let them think I'm sidin' against my own. I figured it was enough for 'em to know I could understand their natterin'."

Connor felt a nauseating wave of guilt flood his soul. It was not merely a matter of foolishness, but he had endangered the whole camp. All the people who had stood by him and Gyorgyike and Gabor had become like an extended family to them, and he had placed them in danger simply by not taking the time to think clearly about what he was doing. "I should have thought about sharing. I honestly don't know why I didn't..." Connor let his voice trail off as Landon's piercing blue eyes bored through to his soul.

"Five dollars says you do know, Connor Slade," he said in a low voice.

Connor knew Landon was not the gambling type. His words were more symbolic than literal, and five dollars was a lot of money to bet on anything. Even as he tried to avoid those piercing eyes, he could not, but the real reason for his treatment of the French trappers became abundantly clear to him. "Yes, I suppose I do," he said, shifting in the saddle.

"You want t' tell me?" Landon suggested, looking ahead to the trail again.

"Not really," Connor replied shortly.

For a while, they rode in silence. The pale blue sky arched overhead, a chilly wind driving some wintry-looking clouds together toward the west.

"They think the whole world belongs to them," Connor said at last, breaking the silence. Not because that silence bothered him, but because it made him feel safe to speak. It was another of the mysteries that was Landon Morland. He could get a feller to talk by simply being quiet. "How many years have we spent building up this land? And they think they can just come in and take over everything we've built. I hate them, you know, the British, French, whoever comes here pretending to be settlers. We're the real settlers, the ones whose parents came here and understood what tyranny is and what freedom is... and gave their lives for that freedom."

Landon made no response while Connor spoke. If he had not known Landon well enough by then, Connor could have been excused for thinking that the man was not listening at all. But he did know Landon very well, after four tough months on the trail, and he knew the wily old rancher was not missing a single word.

"I heard there's a US Army garrison in Fort Vancouver that's taking over the Hudson's Bay Company's headquarters. Since the declaration was signed, those Britons have stuck fast, like ticks in a cow's ear, but our troops are working them out, bit by bit. I want to help them. I want to get rid of the British pigs, get them off our land and back to their little island where they belong."

"Your granddaddy was a British soldier, wasn't he?" Landon asked in a casual tone.

"Yes, he was, until he landed here and realized he was really American at heart. He had freedom in his blood, too, and that's why he deserted from the tyrant's army." Pride coursed hotly through Connor's veins as he spoke.

Landon nodded slowly, his lithe, wiry frame moving in rhythm with his horse's gait. "I ain't here t' taint your granddaddy's memory, nor t' tell ya t' quit hatin' on the British. That's your own row t' hoe. But I will say this: You're part of our little family, now, an' anything you do can hurt us or help us. Once we get over yonder Blue Mountains and we've done survived the Dalles, you can go your merry way an' join up with the US Army. Until then, you'll keep a tight rein on your temper. You owe the rest of us that much, Connor."

Landon's words were true, every single one. Connor swallowed. "Sounds reasonable to me," he replied, thinking what an understatement that was. "Think of the camp first and myself second."

"Yeah," Landon's unemotional response came. "Don't forget, your own wife and child need ya t' think of 'em first, too, before yer pride."

***

Gyorgyike watched Landon and Connor ride back toward the wagon train. Connor looked thoughtful—a little humbled, too, if she was not mistaken. Landon's face was unreadable, as usual. She wondered what their conversation had been about, remembering the French trappers who had come with Connor when he returned from hunting.

"We'll make it to Fort Boise tonight," Landon told the pioneers as he rode down the line.

Gyorgyike would have danced a jig for joy if she had any strength left for dancing. Instead, she smiled up at Gabor, riding on the driver's seat of the wagon. "A few days of rest, my kicsim," she said to him in Hungarian. "That will be like a little piece of heaven."

Gabor gazed back silently at her. She could tell he was happy at the thought, too, though he remained mute, as always. She wondered briefly if he would ever speak. Perhaps in a few years he would at least learn to write and make words with the alphabet. Then she would know for sure if what she believed she was reading in his eyes was what he was thinking.

Connor wheeled his horse around to ride alongside the wagon, and he dismounted, offering the horse to Gyorgyike. She accepted gracefully but without making prolonged eye contact with Connor. He seemed apologetic somehow, but she didn't want him to say anything. She didn't want any kind of scenario to develop where she might feel sympathy or appreciation for him. He was merely doing his duty as a husband.

Sitting aboard the horse, though, a deep gratitude did wash over her, simply for the fact that her feet were no longer required to carry her, and her legs no longer required to propel her forward. Connor hoisted Gabor up onto his shoulders and walked alongside the horse, leading the oxen hitched to the wagon.

"We'll have to trade these for fresh oxen," Connor said, apparently trying to make conversation.

Gyorgyike listened in silence. She had contributed nothing but herself to the marriage, and she felt little inclination to participate in deciding how money should be spent. Connor didn't make any further attempts at communication, and the afternoon passed as so many others had. With the slow plodding of the oxen and the seemingly equally slow sinking of the sun.

Sure enough, just as Landon had predicted, the sun was an hour short of setting when the wagon train crested a rise and the emigrants found themselves staring down at the battlements of Fort Boise. It was surrounded, as all forts along the trail had been, by Indian villages and circled wagon trains. Trappers, like those Connor had come across, wandered in among the crowd with their beaver hats and strings of pelts.

The Snake River wound along the east side of the fort, and the wagon train had to cross over before they could reach the relative safety of the high adobe walls. Gyorgyike noticed a large herd of sheep grazing on a hillside near the fort. Cattle and horses grazed among them, and a neatly tilled vegetable patch about a hundred yards long and a hundred yards wide was surrounded by fences of wood and wire.

It seemed to Gyorgyike that life was going swimmingly for those who manned the fort if they could keep their own little farming operation going. Most of all, she took heart at the sight of what appeared to be an attempt, at least, of normal civilization. Clearly, they were nearing an area where there were more people and more established settlements. Her dream lay tantalizingly within reach.

But the civilized tranquility that seemed to permeate the atmosphere around Fort Boise was quickly shown to be an illusion. The wagon train had scarcely circled at their selected spot when they were beset by a veritable horde of Shoshone and other tribes, all bearing hides they wanted to trade for food, supplies, and whatever else of value they could get their hands on.

Landon had his hands full trying to keep order and translate while the tribes milled about, and the settlers tried to fend them off without offending them. Gyorgyike remembered Landon had warned them many times not to appear apologetic or passive around the Indians.

"They ain't the kind of people t' respect a feller who turns the other cheek. To them, that ain't anything but a sign of weakness. Talk straight to 'em, and they'll respect ya. Just don't insult 'em, that's all."

She hadn't considered that good advice at the time, but after her time with the Shoshone tribe at the Gate of Death, she felt bolder. Standing at the front of the wagon, with Gabor safely inside it and Connor at the rear, she folded her arms over her chest and glared down those who might try to grab something from the wagon and offer a fox pelt or a buffalo robe in return for it.

"Rice!" they cried, "Beans! Sugar!"

Gyorgyike simply shook her head adamantly. They had little, herself having not brought anything along in the way of personal belongings other than the clothes on her and Gabor's back and a few extra outfits. Connor had sold most of what he owned to buy the rig and stow enough cash for the costs they might encounter along the trail. They still had the Barlow Road toll gates to take into consideration, and their funds were already running dangerously low.

Some of the other emigrants, however, were digging through their wagons, looking for any kind of valuable or trinket they might be able to trade for a soft, warm rabbit skin cloak. Billy, especially, seemed to be enjoying the trading frenzy. The Hendersons' wagon was drawn right in front of the Slades'. Gyorgyike, now unmolested since the traders had quickly ascertained who was willing to trade, was treated to a full view of his enthusiastic negotiations.

At one point the boy emerged with a pile of books in his hands. Clambering awkwardly out of the wagon with his prize, he held them up and shouted, "Books! You fellers want books?"

His older brother, Matt, appeared from behind the wagon as if by magic. "Put those back, Billy, they're mine!" he hissed agitatedly.

Billy stopped, looking confused. "Yours? You sure?" He turned the pile of books sideways and peered at the spines. "They're Jane Austen novels. What are you doin' with Jane Austen novels?"

Matt blushed bright red. "They aren't for me to read, silly," he retorted, reaching out to take the books from his little brother's grasp.

Billy jerked them out of his reach. "Who are they for, then?" Billy asked, his eyes bright as he tauntingly held up the books above his head, reveling in Matt's embarrassment as only a younger brother could.

"If you must know, they're for Carrie, but don't you dare tell her. I know she likes to read those kinds of novels, and I found them in an abandoned chest down in the Rockies." Matt glanced around, and Gyorgyike pretended to be interested in another trade going on at the bachelors' wagon.

"How come you ain't given 'em to her yet, if they're for her?" Billy questioned teasingly. "I reckon you've been readin' 'em on the sly."

"No," Matt insisted emphatically. "I just haven't had the nerve to give them to her yet. It's kind of an important gift, you know? I have to give it to her at the right time…"

Gyorgyike didn't hear the rest of the conversation. Her thoughts were consumed with the sweet tenderness of Matt toward Carrie, the Morlands' oldest daughter. No man had ever been that sweet to her. Not that she knew of. She wondered if Connor had ever wanted to give her a gift but held back, fearful of her rejection.

Quickly shoving the thought from her mind, she reminded herself once more of her mission. To be independent, unfettered by a man and free to make her own choices. She could not allow emotions to get in the way of her purpose and plan for her life. Not when she was getting so, so close.

# Chapter 7
# Fort Boise

The few days of rest at Fort Boise was a welcome reprieve for the exhausted pioneers. After the trading frenzy, which later repeated itself on other wagon trains that arrived in subsequent days, they all settled into the routine of doing repairs, stocking up on provisions that were running low, and catching up on the latest news from the locals.

Landon took Clyde, Noel, and Connor with him when he went to see the commander in charge of the fort, as had become his habit at every fort they stopped at. Connor felt honored that Landon still took him along, considering he had placed the entire wagon train in danger with his impetuous behavior. The gesture bolstered his firm resolve to use a whole lot more good judgment when he was faced with unexpected situations in the future.

The fort was owned and run by the British Hudson's Bay Company, which did not bode well for Connor. As the four men walked together toward the entrance of the fort, he mentally prepared himself to keep a watch on his mouth and only open it when necessary to say things like, "Yes, sir," or, "No, sir." He was still deep in thought, conjuring up possible scenarios that might arise fueled by the undoubted arrogance of the British officer in charge, when the sound of boots pounding on the rocky earth plucked him from his imaginings.

Connor turned in unison with his companions to see three men running toward the same entrance they were headed for, carrying a fourth man covered in blood, his head lolling back on the shoulder of one of his companions.

"Make way! Make way!" they were shouting, their faces drawn and pale with worry.

Connor and his companions were almost at the gate of the fort, but they stepped aside and let the frantic party pass ahead of them.

"I sure hope he survives," Clyde said, gazing after them.

It was with a somber air hanging around them that the four emigrants waited outside the fort commander's office. A man emerged from the office after a few minutes and yelled an order to another man, intimating that, "Craigie needs a basin of hot water and some towels," and that the man should, "get a move on." He stopped to look at the four emigrants standing outside the office and blinked. "Anything I can do for you gentlemen?" he asked.

"We came t' see the commander of the fort," Landon replied, fulfilling his role of group spokesman.

"Ah, well, he's a little tied up at the moment, as you can see," the man informed them unnecessarily. "Fellow shot himself in the shoulder by accident, dragging his shotgun out of his wagon by the barrel, if you can imagine that. I don't know how so many of you Yankees have made it this far, even. Although, Doctor McLoughlin says you lot could go right over to China with your wagons if you desired to do it."

Connor stared at him blankly. He hadn't been called a Yankee to his face yet, and he hadn't anticipated how it might make him feel. Strangely enough, he found he felt quite proud of the epithet that so many British folk used as a bit of a slur.

"I reckon we could if we had a mind to," Landon remarked, humor twitching at the corners of his mouth. Then he reverted to the issue at hand. "I ain't supposin' this feller's gunshot wound is goin' t' take a short while, is it?" he postured.

"Oh, don't you worry, sir. James Craigie is a dab hand with anything and everything. He'll patch him up in no time and be ready to see you before you can say knife."

Without waiting for a response, the man dodged back inside the office, and Connor and his friends were once again left standing outside on the porch, wondering what to do with themselves. In true British style, the definition of "no time" turned out to be rather more than a few minutes, but at last the man emerged once more, holding the door for the injured overlander and his three helpers to exit.

Connor felt grateful such a fate had not befallen one of them as yet, a fact he could only attribute to Landon's presence at the helm of their fleet of prairie schooners. He had made sure that everyone who owned and operated a firearm of any kind first had a rigorous test, designed by himself, and when they failed on any part of the test, he had taken it upon himself to educate them until they were all proficient gun handlers and marksmen.

Entering the office of the Hudson's Bay Company's employee filled him with an entirely different feeling. This was basically the enemy's lair. Every instinct in him told him to keep his hand ready at his holster, but the memory of his promise to Landon to think before reacting still held strong sway over his emotions. He looked at the man behind the fort commander's desk with trepidation.

James Craigie was a tall man, with narrow shoulders, a long, oval face covered with neatly trimmed, sandy whiskers. His eyes, slightly narrowed and creased with smile lines, were a startling blue and seemed to twinkle with mischief and kindness at the same time. He wore a cloth cap made of green and gray tartan with finer stripes of red and black and sipped thoughtfully on a glass of what appeared to be whiskey as he regarded his latest visitors.

"Well, good morning, gentlemen," he said with a distinctive Gaelic lilt in his accent, accentuated with slightly rolled r's. What was most noticeable to Connor, though, was that his tone held none of the condescending disdain some of the British people at Fort Hall had displayed. "I'm so sorry for the delay. As you must have seen, I had a rather pressing matter to deal with, but thankfully that is out of the way for the moment. How may I be of assistance?"

Connor was glad he wasn't the one speaking with the fort commander. He felt quite tongue-tied and would have floundered about like the stranded salmon they had tossed out onto the pebbled beaches of the Snake River so many times. Countless stories had been told about how unhelpful and downright rude the managers were at Fort Boise, as well as every other fort from then on westward, but James Craigie was the compete opposite of every projection Connor had made.

It was not without reason that he had that impression. Even after the boundary treaty had been signed four years prior, the Hudson's Bay Company had held on grimly to their trading posts that had once been forts, establishing their part in the joint occupation of the Oregon Territory.

There were many tales told of how HBC employees, all the way to the upper echelons, had done everything in their power to dissuade the overlanders from completing their journey. One tactic was withholding assistance when the overlanders were in trouble. Another was buying their last earthly possessions off them for a song once they reached their destination, leaving them with very little to build a new life with.

Instead, this man appeared to be the epitome of helpfulness and compassion. Connor couldn't remember a Briton aiding a pioneer who had injured himself in any way, let alone a shotgun accident that could be waved off as careless and the poor victim left to wallow in his just desserts. He felt a little uncomfortable, thinking of his fervent desire to rid the land of the European scum when one of them was looking at him and his companions with such blatant goodwill.

"We were wonderin' if you could give us any advice regardin' the trail from here t' the Dalles," Landon was saying when Connor dragged his attention back to the conversation.

"Well, I'm not sure I'm the man to give you any reliable information on that part of the trail," James Craigie said, tapping his fingertips together. "I've been in and out of the fort and not much in touch with goings on outside of it. Only this year I came to oversee things permanently, so I'm still finding my feet, if you will." His eyes creased up even more as he smiled at them. "But I can tell you this: Don't dally. Make sure you take enough provisions and move whenever you can. And when you get to Oregon City, call on Doctor John McLoughlin. You can tell him I sent you. He'll make sure you get a decent plot of land and decent prices for whatever you want to sell."

"I've heard of him," Landon said slowly.

"I'm sure you have. He's made quite a name for himself already. Let's just say he's as little enamored with our dear company's treatment of the locals as I am. The news of how Americans were being treated is what compelled me to station myself here permanently. I had to see for myself what was going on, you understand?"

Connor stared at the man.

"I dare say, it seems foolhardy to walk all over the very people who could mean our livelihood, or lack of it, in a few years' time. I've quite taken to the idea, the same that Dr. McLoughlin has, of becoming a naturalized American as soon as I am able. The way your people have forged relentlessly across this unforgiving land is a testament to a kind of spirit I think we've lost in England. We're far more concerned with downright petty issues, now that we don't have to fight off wolves and bears and Vikings anymore." He gave a little chuckle. "But don't let me ramble on and on. How are your animals holding up? We have a few rested, fatted creatures you could trade out, though I do believe it will be unlikely you'll be able to make a straight swap."

"We've heard we can get one fat animal for two thin, trail-weary ones," Connor piped up, remembering his grandfather defecting to the side of the Revolutionaries almost three-quarters of a century before. There was a war of a different kind going on in his lifetime, but there were clearly still Britons like his old grandpa around. He hoped there would be more, though he wasn't about to hold his breath.

"Yes, that is the going trade price at the moment, I'm afraid. What I can do is toss in a sheep or two into the deal. At least you'll have meat on the hoof for a couple of weeks," Craigie offered.

"Well, that's mighty kind of ya, sir," Landon said, nodding to show his gratitude. "I reckon there's a few of us who won't mind takin' you up on that offer."

"Then it's settled," Craigie agreed and stood to his feet. "If there's anything else, we can discuss it on the way to your camp."

Thanks to the kindness of Mr. Craigie, the trades were made, and the pioneers' supplies and provisions stocked up in readiness for the long haul to the Dalles. And a long haul it was.

"There's not a fort or a settlement from here until the other side of the Blue Mountains," Craigie warned them. "Beware of the Cayuse, they have an ax to grind with white folk, so you'll want to steer clear of them if you can. The Walla Walla are quite the opposite, though."

"Thank you kindly, Mr. Craigie," Landon said with genuine gratitude in his voice. "We sure won't forget your kindness, sir. It's been a pleasure knowin' ya."

The two men shook hands warmly, and Connor decided that the Scots in the British ranks were fellows he could get along with. Still, he was convinced people like Craigie were in the minority, and he mentally reinforced his decision to join up with the army at Fort Vancouver.

The next day, before sunrise, the overlanders hitched up their oxen, mounted their horses, and headed out for the next leg of their journey. The older children were excited about the handful of sheep that had now joined the ranks of livestock and enthusiastically drove them on beside the wagons. Even Gabor and Fiona joined in for a while, their stubby four-year-old legs pumping madly until they could go no further.

Connor looked at his new, lone ox pulling the wagon. The animal seemed to be straining hard against the yoke, its sinews standing out on its well-fleshed body. He looked up at Gyorgyike who was taking the first turn riding their horse for the day. "I have a feeling this feller isn't going to make it, pulling this wagon all by himself," he remarked, not really expecting a reply.

"I was thinking the same thing," Gyorgyike's answer surprised him.

"What d'you suppose we could do to help? Lighten the load?" Connor gladly grasped the tidbit of connection between himself and his reticent wife.

"There is not much more we can throw out," she said, shaking her head.

At that moment, the children came past the wagon driving the livestock to the front of the train. Maybelle, the Slades' milk cow, looked peeved at being rushed along, but she had little choice in the matter. The children were determined to get the livestock up ahead again so they could stop and graze a while until the wagon train passed by once more. Not that there was much grazing around. The animals were reduced chiefly to browsing on the sagebrush that had become steadily more profuse as they drew further away from Fort Boise. Connor watched the beasts shambling off into the distance with the children whooping and hollering at their heels.

"What about Maybelle?" Gyorgyike asked out of the blue.

Connor turned his head to look up at her, not sure what she meant. "Maybelle? Our milk cow?" he asked.

"Yah, she is still strong, no?"

"I suppose she is. She looks all right," Connor replied, wondering where Gyorgyike's train of thought was going.

"What if we yoke her in wit' the ox?"

Connor stared at her, wondering why he hadn't thought of that. He had just never seen the little Jersey cow as anything more than a supply of milk for Gabor and butter for them. "I believe you have an idea worth trying, there," he said, smiling up at her.

Gyorgyike looked away to the front of the wagon train. "Maybe at nooning we can yoke her in and see if that will work."

"Sure, let's do that," Connor agreed, still smiling, but Gyorgyike studiously avoided eye contact with him. Connor squashed the feelings of frustration that rose in his chest. He had to take the small steps forward with the seemingly giant steps back. Maybe when they were settled in a little homestead in Oregon City or near the army barracks, she would soften without the rigors of the trail wearing her down.

And the rigors were by no means letting up yet. They were leaving behind the exhausting, rock-strewn trail of the Rockies and the Snake River, constantly beset with river crossings and steep, narrow passes, and for that Connor was grateful. He knew he was not the only one, too. But slowly the truth became apparent that this section of the trail was not free of trials. It merely presented discomforts unique to itself.

The sage brush increased in size and number until they were wading through veritable forests of it growing as high as their shoulders. Grass was almost nonexistent, and the rocks had given way to fine dust that rose up and seemed to hang in the air for hours.

The sun beat down mercilessly during the day, and water was in short supply. Whenever they reached a stream that fed the Snake River still flowing by a few miles to their right, they made sure to fill up as many containers as they could. Some of the men had cleaned out the hollow horn taken from ox carcasses along the way, and they became very useful water canteens.

As they had done on the prairies, the emigrants fanned out, each wagon taking a different track to avoid walking in the dust trail of the wagon ahead. Three distinct swales were already scored into the dry earth, evidence that others before them had used the same strategy. Still, the dust managed to get everywhere, including in their nostrils, ears, and eyes. With water so scarce, it was impossible to wash their faces more than twice a day.

After the first week or so of complaining, eventually they learned to live with it, although it grew more difficult not to complain after the trail turned more west than north and veered away from the Snake River. With water becoming even scarcer, spirits began to flag more and more.

The milk cow didn't much like being yoked alongside the ox and pulling a heavy wagon day in and day out, but there was no room for man or beast to get cantankerous about personal preferences. Soon enough she began to accept her lot, although the amount of milk Connor managed to coax from her each morning and evening was becoming decidedly less.

After nearly two weeks of trudging through what felt like an endless sea of sagebrush, Connor led Maybelle and the ox up a steep ridge and drew in a breath of wonder. Below them, a vast valley spread out as flat as a tabletop. Beyond it, an imposing line of hazy blue mountains lay swathed in mist.

"There they are," Connor said, feeling his spirits lift at the sight of the landmark. "The Blue Mountains. On the other side of those lies the land of promise."

Gyorgyike didn't reply, but when Connor looked at her, her eyes seemed to shine a little, in a way he hadn't seen before. That simple sight set his spirits soaring even higher.

Perhaps he had been right. Perhaps all she needed was some creature comforts and what now felt like a luxury: staying in one place for more than three or four days. If he could just hold out until they were settled for a while, she might surprise them both and learn to love him.

# Chapter 8
# Cayuse

"I never thought these mountains would be so easy to cross," Connor remarked to Landon as they rode ahead to scout the trail on the fourth day across the second to last barrier that separated them from their new life in Oregon.

"Five dollars says you wouldn't have said that walkin' straight into these mountains from Boston," Landon chuckled dryly.

"You have a point, captain," Connor confessed, laughing. "After trudging through the Rockies, though, I suppose my perspective on what's hard and what's easy has changed a little."

"Just a little?" Landon asked, sarcasm thick in his tone despite his characteristic lack of facial expressions.

"All right, then, a whole lot," Connor admitted before continuing to remark on the mountains they were traversing. "These are really just a lot of oversized hills, don't you think?"

"I reckon you could call 'em that." Landon nodded, but Connor could see the wheels turning in his mind. "Thing is, these tame puppies grow a lot of nasty teeth when winter sets in, and that ain't a lie."

"I heard tell about a family of children who lost both their parents and came through here too late to miss the snows. Seems they nearly died of cold before a local missionary found them," Connor said, scanning the rounded domes of the mountains around him and wondering what they might look like covered with snow. As it was, everything looked pretty much the same, just wave after wave of rolling giant hills. It would be quite impossible to know which way you were going if it was all covered in an icy white blanket.

"Yeah, the Sager children. T' think that was just six years ago," Landon said thoughtfully. "They crossed the Blues quite a way up north from here. Got taken in by the Whitmans. Good people, so I hear. Such a pity how they got massacred by the Cayuse."

"They got massacred?" Connor echoed in horror, remembering James Craigie's warning about the Cayuse nation.

"You recall Craigie said they got an ax to grind with white folk?"

Connor nodded, watching Landon scouting out the countryside even as he spoke.

"Folks tell different stories about why they killed all them missionaries, but by all accounts, they believed they were being poisoned."

"They thought the missionaries were poisoning them?" Connor asked, seeking clarity on the mindset of the tribe he hoped they wouldn't run into on their journey across the Blue Mountains.

"That's how the story goes," Landon said.

"I reckon we'll just stick to, 'don't shoot till you're shot at,' then, right?"

"That'll be the safest bet. Always is unless you know you're in a duel." Once again, Landon's practicality hit the nail right on the head.

One thing they couldn't escape was the fact it was getting decidedly colder now: they were rising in elevation, and the first tinges of red, yellow, and orange were showing on the cottonwoods, vine maples, and aspens. There were even a few strange fir trees with their needles turning golden yellow to signal the changing seasons.

As fascinating as that was to the children, the adults knew that falling leaves heralded the steadily approaching winter, and with the second week of October already rolling by them, the scent of snow was heavy in the air.

Connor, taking heart from his conversation with Gyorgyike about yoking Maybelle alongside the ox, made more attempts than usual to yoke his wife to his company but with little success. The frustration ate at him until he confided in Landon one day while they were riding up front to scout the trail.

"A woman is like a wild critter," Landon said, his voice matter of fact. "You can put 'em in a cage, but they'll stay wild, and they'll likely never trust ya. Best is t' let 'em come to you. Thing is, you got t' know what they like so you can draw 'em in. A feller could call it bait, I reckon, though ya might not keep yer head on yer shoulders if ya ever say so in front of a lady."

Connor laughed. The image in his mind seemed even more comical than it might have been in the light of

Landon's serious visage as he made the unthinkable comparison. "If I only knew what bait to use, my pursuit might be a little easier," Connor lamented, thinking how true Landon's words were.

"If you listen well enough, you'll know what's nearest and dearest to her heart. That's the bait you'll be needin'."

Connor nodded. He let his mind wander as they rode along, checking for anything suspicious or any problems with the trail. What was it Gyorgyike loved more than anything else in the world? The question had scarcely crossed his mind when the answer became clear to him.

*Of course! Gabor!* Her little boy was her life, and she doted upon him with the simultaneously tender and fierce devotion of a mother bear. That was clear enough to Connor. He himself was very fond of the little chap and, whenever Gyorgyike was not around, he had tried to connect with the boy. It suddenly seemed logical to build a strong relationship with his little stepson. As much as Gabor's muteness would allow, that is.

For the next few days, instead of merely waiting for opportunities to present themselves as he had before, Connor sought time to spend with his stepson. Gabor seemed quite happy to oblige, and Connor felt a deep sense of fulfillment that he had not expected. But the best discovery came when he followed Gabor and Fiona and watched the two friends playing near a stream they had stopped at for nooning.

The two children were picking up pebbles and tossing them into the rippling waters, squealing with delight at the plop and splash as each one went in. Progressing from small pebbles to larger and larger ones, the game escalated to almost a frenzy.

"Stop, Gabi. Mama said not to get wet," Fiona said after the two had convulsed in gales of laughter at a large splash created by a large pebble tossed into the water by Gabor.

"Okay, Fee," Gabor said, dropping the equally large stone he had picked up.

For a moment, Connor didn't realize what had happened. Then Fiona spoke again.

"Can you throw the stone across the river?"

Gabor nodded vigorously. "Can throw across!" he exclaimed, picking up another, smaller pebble and hurling it with all his might.

The stone plopped into the water, and the two children were once more consumed with laughter. As Connor joined in, a thought struck him. Gabor had responded to Fiona with words. A little stilted and poorly articulated, but words, nonetheless.

He stopped mid-guffaw and stared at the boy. "You can speak, Gabor?" he asked, stunned.

Gabor looked at him with his wide, black eyes and blinked.

"He speaks to me, Mister Slade," Fiona said. "All the time." She picked up a pebble and flung it with all her might, but hers also plopped into the middle of the stream and disappeared beneath the rushing waters.

"Too short!" Gabor shouted, jumping up and down.

"Did you tell his mama?" Connor asked Fiona.

She shook her head, looking as if she was trying to figure out why that would be necessary, and then turned to pick up another pebble to fling across the stream.

"You do not know what you've done, do you, little angel?"

Connor watched the two children playing until Nellie, the Hendersons' oldest daughter, was sent to call them to come and eat. The little ones' playing had certainly bolstered their appetites, and they dropped what they were doing and complied immediately.

Connor followed along behind them, still trying to absorb what he had just witnessed. It was a miracle. A child who had not spoken his entire life was saying words and short, if disjointed, sentences. And all because a little girl had not accepted the impediment as part of who he was.

He knew Fiona to be a little chatterbox. She would have just kept on at him, peppering him with her endless questions, and eventually he would have had to make some kind of verbal response. Adults had just given up on him too quickly. That was all Connor could put it down to.

That night, when the pioneers deserted their shared evening fire one by one to retire for a night of well-earned rest, Connor waited until it left only Clyde playing gentle lullabies on his violin. Landon sat contemplating the dying embers of the fire, lost in his own thoughts, before he said something about what he had seen and heard at the stream that day.

Gyorgyike was scratching out patterns in the loose, dry earth with a stick, and she started a little when Connor spoke to her, as if she had forgotten he was even there. It affected him more than he let on, knowing she stayed up longer than most simply to avoid being alone with him in the wagon for too many hours of the night. Gabor was already bedded down and sleeping under a throw made of rabbit pelts Dearbhla had given them.

"You won't believe this, Gyorgyike," Connor said in a low voice, not really wanting to attract the attention of the other two men. "But Gabor is talking. I heard him myself today, talking to Fiona."

After her initial fright, and the words had sunk in, Gyorgyike looked at him, dumbfounded. "He has never said a word to me, not a word. How is he speaking to this child?" she asked incredulously, her own voice barely above a whisper.

"That's the miracle," Connor replied, shrugging but unable to stop the grin spreading across his face. "She must have just kept at him until he answered her one day, and then that was that."

Gyorgyike went back to scratching out patterns in the dirt. "What did he say?" she asked, still sounding a little skeptical, but her curiosity clearly getting the better of her.

"Just short little phrases. Oh, gosh, I don't remember exactly. Like, 'too short' was one and 'can throw across' I think. Things like that." Connor felt elated that he could be the one to tell her that her son was breaking his silence, that there was hope he would one day call her Mama.

"If this is true, why does he not speak to me?" she insisted, sounding agitated.

Connor's heart sank. Things were not going as he had envisaged. Not that he had expected her to fling her arms around his neck and tell him he was her hero, but he had at least hoped she would believe him. "I don't know," Connor countered, trying not to let his emotions run away with him. "All I know is that I heard him speak to Fiona."

"Did he speak to you?" Gyorgyike asked, still not looking up from her stick, scratching away by her feet.

"No, not a word. I asked if he was speaking, and he ignored me completely, just chattered away to Fiona. Called her Fee, now that I think about it. She told me he talks to her all the time. Seemed surprised that I was asking if he could speak." He spoke as unemotionally as he could, despite the excitement bubbling inside him.

Gyorgyike seemed mollified by his answer, but she said nothing more. The silence grew into a great, yawning chasm between them until Clyde and Landon grunted their goodnights and wandered off to their respective wagons. Connor waited until Gyorgyike had followed their lead and was in the wagon a few minutes before he made his way to retire for the night.

He lay awake, staring at the grayness of the canvas above him in the darkness. *One step forward, two steps back,* he thought morosely, *and it sure doesn't feel like an Irish jig to me.*

By the time morning rolled around, he had decided not to try too hard, not to expect anything. The disappointment he was bound to feel was just not worth it. Instead, he focused his attention on Gabor and the livestock. They, at least, appreciated his efforts.

He was riding the horse alongside the wagon, with Gabor sitting on the front of the saddle with him when Brady came galloping up along the wagon train, waving his hat. "Circle the wagons! Circle the wagons!" he called out frantically.

The pioneers had learned that when Brady called out anything like that, it was a good idea to follow his advice. The young man, though sometimes a little brash and cocksure, never cried wolf unless there really was one.

As the emigrants hastily drew their wagons into a circle, Landon appeared, also riding hard. "It's Cayuse," he explained shortly. "We saw 'em first, and we tried t' get away unnoticed, but they spotted us. They're headed this way. Every man of you get your firin' irons ready. Ladies and boys who can shoot, do the same, but don't anybody pull a trigger before my say so."

The men ran for their guns, filling their pockets with ammunition and slinging their powder horns over their shoulders. The women and older children hid the youngsters in among the barrels of provisions in the wagons. At least that way there was less chance of them getting shot. Everyone who could shoot held their guns ready.

A moment later, the Cayuse appeared. They did not look at all like most of the warriors Connor had seen. Dressed in what looked like deer hide pants and shirts, fringed, and beaded, they looked as if they were headed to a wedding, not intent on war. They had not painted their faces, either, but Connor thought it would not have made much difference to how frightening they looked.

Their faces wore an expression of such aggression that it made Connor's stomach turn. He shuddered involuntarily. As they bore down on the circled wagons, apparently not caring that the emigrants might have guns pointing at their chests, they emitted a coarse, guttural cry, which sounded nothing like the whoops and shrieks Connor expected, while they rode around and around the emigrants.

A growing sense of unrest filled him, and he felt the trigger under his finger seem to grow hot, as if it had been engulfed in flames for more than a few minutes. In silence, the emigrants watched the Cayuse approach, and then suddenly one warrior let out a shrill whoop, then he took aim with the sawn-off shotgun in his hand and blasted off a round.

A cry erupted from behind Connor. "He hit me in the leg!" It sounded like Arthur Riley, the other Bostonian of the group.

"Get ready, fellers," Landon's deep, confident tones rang out. "We may need t' fight for our families today."

As he spoke, another shot rang out, this time from a younger Cayuse. A shower of dust sprang up at Connor's feet, and he pulled them in, but before he could refocus, another shot rang out, and he heard the bullet whistle past his ear.

"Fire if ya need t', fellers!" Landon ordered.

Connor looked up to see the barrel of a large old musket pointed at him. With hardly a thought going through his mind, he lifted his rifle and fired. The Cayuse jerked sideways and fell from his horse. Connor didn't see what happened to him after that. The air was suddenly full of gunfire and shouting. It was all he could do to keep his focus on the horsemen thundering by, their weapons pointed at him or others behind him.

In the confusion, he could hardly make out when it was one of their own who cried out in pain or one of their attackers. All he could do was man his spot and try to keep the enemy out of the little huddle of people who had become his family in the last five odd months. Firing and reloading, firing, and reloading, one eye always on the men riding past, round and around until it felt like there were hundreds of them.

It filled the air with the smell of gun smoke, sweat, dust, and blood. Connor's heart beat in his ears, and still not a lucid thought crossed his mind. All he was aware of was a desire to survive, to remain unscathed if possible, and to protect those he cared for from being killed or injured.

After what felt like an interminable time, the Cayuse appeared to decide this pocket of determined pioneers was not worth the loss of their men. One particularly fierce-looking warrior called out something in their language, and the warriors began to peel away, one by one, and disappear into the mountains. Some stopped to hoist their dead or injured onto the back of their horses before they rode away.

As he watched them go, Connor held his finger, still ready over the trigger of his Colt. An eerie silence descended on the group. Connor's ears were ringing. His eyes stung from sweat and smoke, but he did not move. Who knew if they had really left? They could just as easily be regrouping just beyond the rise.

Slowly, sounds filtered through the ringing in Connor's ears. The moaning of injured men and the whimpering of children. The wailing of a woman. A distant roll of thunder. For a long while, Connor remained crouched behind his wagon, but the Cayuse did not return. Slowly, he looked around.

They stretched Arthur Riley out behind his wagon, his left trouser leg a mess of blood and torn cloth. His wife, Lorna, sat with his head in her lap, rocking back and forth while she moaned and sobbed inconsolably. Connor felt a lump rise in his throat. Lorna was clearly a widow, now, and she had dearly loved the man who lay dead on the ground beside her. For a fleeting moment, Connor wished he could have been taken instead. He didn't have a wife who would mourn his passing, not the way Lorna mourned Arthur's.

# Chapter 9
# Sacrifice

Gyorgyike's hands trembled as she lowered the revolver. It had been more difficult to point a firearm at a living, breathing human than she had imagined, even the large, angry man intent on doing her harm that she had just faced. A life was still a life, and she could not bring herself to take another as much as that person might deserve to be cut short. She wiped her eyes with her apron, fighting back the confusion and shock.

Peering around her through the smoke and dust, she saw Connor still crouched behind their wagon, his eyes fixed on the direction the Cayuse had disappeared into. He seemed to expect them to come back. Gyorgyike didn't care if they were coming back or not. She needed to check on Gabor and reassure him.

Quickly, she clambered into the wagon. Her little boy was still curled up in the fetal position between the wooden barrels and boxes, sucking his thumb. He looked up at her, his eyes wide, and she saw his face was tear-streaked even though she had not heard a single sound out of him the entire time.

"It's okay, my kicsim," she reassured him in Hungarian. "We're safe now. The wicked men got a big fright because we fought them off. Don't you worry, they won't be back if they know what's good for them. Here, let Mama dry your eyes."

She held her arms out to him, and he scrambled into her embrace, seeking solace. For a while they stayed like that while Gyorgyike rocked him back and forth, and then she lifted him up onto her hip and clambered out of the wagon. The first thing she saw was Lorna Riley bending over the motionless form of her husband, her hands smeared with bright red blood.

"I tried to stop the bleeding," she was saying, her voice as shaky as her blood-covered hands. "But I just couldn't. It just kept coming, no matter how much or how hard I pressed and pressed…" Her voice trailed off into sobs.

Gyorgyike held Gabor's face against her shoulder so he would not look around and see the bloodstained left thigh of the late Arthur Riley. The shotgun blast seemed to have hit him on the inside of the leg, and the entire area was a glistening mess.

Anna, Clyde, and Landon had already gathered around Lorna. Anna did what she could to console the bereaved woman, while Landon gave orders for one of the nearest bystanders to bring a sheet. Clyde closed Arthur's staring, sightless eyes. Louise, Landon's wife, arrived with a basin of water and washed the blood from the still weeping Lorna's hands.

Gyorgyike felt her heart ache. Here was just one more reason not to allow Connor close, especially emotionally, and he had been making that very difficult lately. It could just as well have been him lying there in a pool of blood. She knew it would have meant her freedom, instantly, and yet she felt grateful it was not him.

Thrusting the thought aside, she carried Gabor over to the Tanners' wagon, where Dearbhla was binding up a wound on Noel's arm. Fiona peeped out from behind the canvas cover of the wagon, and she looked relieved when she saw Gyorgyike approaching with Gabor in her arms.

The two children embraced silently, and Gyorgyike wondered once more about what Connor had told her the night before. But there was no time to ask questions about Gabor talking to his best friend. Landon was calling everyone together, and they huddled in the middle of the camp, all the men still armed and ready with their guns, their eyes darting back to the surrounding prairie.

"We got two choices," Landon was saying as Gyorgyike drew close, along with Dearbhla and Noel and the children. "We could stay here an' wait to see if they come back, or we could move out fast as we can t' get further away from their territory."

"What's the best choice, cap'n?" Noel piped up dryly.

Landon gave a wry smirk. "Afraid ain't one that's better than the other. If we stay here, they know where we are, and they'll find us easy. If we haul on out, they could be watchin' us, just waitin' for us to break formation an' lay ourselves bare for easy pickin's."

"You're right," Clyde remarked, nodding in his slow, deliberate manner. "Neither of those are great choices, but we'll have to pick one and know what we're about quickly."

"I could scout and see if they're still around, Pa," Brady spoke up, his mouth set in a grim line.

Landon hesitated. It seemed to Gyorgyike that he was a father in that moment, much the same way she was a mother. If Brady had been her son, she would never have let him go out on his own to trail the Cayuse to see where they were going, no matter how silently he could stalk deer and prairie dogs. War-hungry Cayuse were not the same thing.

However, to her surprise, she saw Landon give a single curt nod. "All right then," he agreed, "but you'd better not get too close. Trail 'em until you can see where they are from a distance, then you get yourself back here lickety-split and let us know."

"Sure thing, Pa," Brady said. There was none of the foolhardy, childish bravado that one might have expected from one his age given such a task. It was clear he knew how dangerous the mission was. But there was also an unspoken understanding among the settlers. Men who were not married would leave no widows or orphans, and so they left the most dangerous jobs for them.

"I'll go with you, Brady," Matt volunteered, stepping up beside his friend.

But Brady shook his head. "You're too clumsy, Matt. They'll hear us comin' a mile off." He grinned at his fellow youth and then quickly sobered up again. "Besides, I need ya here t' look after Carrie for me since Pa'll be takin' care of Ma and the young 'uns."

Matt flushed a little, but nodded resolutely. "I'll surely do my best," he promised, squaring his jaw.

Brady turned and left without another word, following the trail the Cayuse had taken. With his departure, the eerie silence descended on the camp once more. There was nothing to do, really, except wait and watch. The men were restless, each one still holding their revolvers and rifles ready. They either sat on the wagon tongues and cast fearful glances toward the hills round about them or paced up and down, doing the same.

Gyorgyike watched the children playing a whispered game of scotch-hoppers. She wished she could join in. At least she would have something other than the mounting breathless tension to focus on. She envied the children their ability to play a game and allow themselves even whispered laughter in the gathering shadow of death.

Gyorgyike tried not to look at the blanket-covered heap that used to be Arthur Riley. They would have to bury him soon, but it didn't seem right to dig a hole right then and there. A hollow feeling invaded the pit of her stomach. Death was suddenly closer than she had ever seen it before, and it was nothing like the caricature that popular culture liked to dress it up as.

After what felt like hours, the scrambling of boots and the sound of Brady's voice could be heard. "I'm back, Pa," he called out as he approached, clearly aware there were many twitchy trigger fingers in the camp who wouldn't hesitate to shoot at any sound or movement that wasn't easily identifiable.

Landon strode quickly toward the sound of his son's voice. "Get in here quick, son. Tell us what you saw," he commanded.

"Oh, praise be to God, you made it back safely," Anna Henderson said, clasping her hands together.

"They've joined up with their village again, a few miles northeast of us. Looks to me like they're havin' a bit of a shindig or somethin'. There's a lot of food bein' cooked, an' the men doin' all sorts of ridin' and shootin' competitions with each other. I reckon we should move outta here fast as we can, get further up the trail, an' away from them. They ain't likely t' bother us this mornin', from what I can see, anyhow."

Landon nodded vigorously. Taking not more than a few seconds to process his son's report, he cleared his throat. "Right, folks, you heard the lad. Let's get movin'."

Under Landon's brisk exhortation, the circle of wagons became a line once more, and the emigrants were on their way again. Looking over their shoulders, they resisted the urge to push their tired beasts harder than was necessary. Losing an ox, or a dairy cow yoked in with the ox, could just as easily mean their deaths as being caught from behind by the battle-thirsty Cayuse tribe.

By the time nooning arrived, they had made what felt like good progress, and there were no further signs of Cayuse around. Circling the wagons near a creek, the women went to fetch water from the nearby stream while the men dug a hole for Arthur Riley's burial.

As she stooped down at the stream to fill the water canteens she had brought along, Gyorgyike noticed movement across from her in the rocky brushwood on the opposite bank of the stream. In a flash, she stood erect, her hand reaching into her dress pocket for the spare revolver she was still carrying, her fingers already tingling with fear.

She looked into the wide, dark brown eyes of a beautiful, round-faced woman. Her pitch-black, silky hair was already graying around her temples, but her dark olive skin seemed like that of a twenty-year-old.

"I do not hurt you. I come to fetch water, too," she said, her voice rippling like the water in the stream between them as the woman stepped out from the trees and underbrush, carrying two large canteens of her own.

"Who are you? What do you want?" Gyorgyike asked, not ready to trust anyone before they had proven themselves, no matter how benign they might seem on the surface.

"Who're you talkin' to, Willow?" a gruff male voice broke in before the woman could reply, and Gyorgyike stared, wide-eyed, as a tall, lanky man dressed in stained brown deer hide, with a graying brown beard and a beaver hat pulled low over his forehead stepped into view. As soon as he saw her, he stopped in his tracks, his own eyes stretching wide beneath his bushy gray eyebrows. "Well, well, well! Visitors, eh? We ain't had any of those in a while!" he exclaimed happily, his leathery, lined features breaking into a gap-toothed grin.

"We are just stopping for nooning. We will be gone soon," Gyorgyike assured him, wondering if his intentions were good.

The man came to stand beside the woman and put an arm around her. "Me and Willow, here, we'd love some company, wouldn't we, honey? I know you folks on the trail have little in the way of vittles, so if you'd like, you could share some of our stew. We put a big pot on today. Well,

Willow did. She said there would be people wantin' it, she just didn't know who."

Gyorgyike didn't know how to respond to that. It seemed too complicated for her mind to process successfully. Suddenly, a hand on her shoulder made her jump, and Connor's voice sounded in her ear.

"Well, that's mighty kind of you, mister," he said. "We were just about to bury one of our own. Got shot by Cayuse just this morning. I'm sure a wonderful stew would comfort if you've any to spare."

"Sure! Sure! Plenty t' spare," the old man assured him, but his grin had faded. "I'm sure sorry t' hear about your friend, though. Nasty business that, an' all started because one son of a gun figured it was a good idea t' tell a lie."

"Tell a lie?" Connor asked, sounding as nonplussed as Gyorgyike felt.

"I'll tell ya the complete story when we bring the stew," the man said, waving off Connor's curiosity. "By the way, the name's William Travis. Y'all can call me Will."

"All right, Will," Connor replied, doffing his hat. "We're just up the slope a ways."

The old man nodded and disappeared into the undergrowth. Willow smiled gently, albeit rather sadly from what Gyorgyike could tell, and stepped down to the water to fill her canteens. Gyorgyike followed suit and returned to the camp with Connor.

When they got there, Arthur was already covered by a mound of earth and large rocks that the men had rolled over his grave to keep the wolves and coyotes out. Landon took off his hat and gave a short eulogy and an even shorter prayer. Lorna wept into a large white handkerchief, while Anna stood arm in arm with her and stroked the bereaved woman's hand.

The funeral was over in a matter of minutes, punctuated by Will and Willow bearing their offering of stew. It was a wonderful stew, better than Gyorgyike had tasted in a long time. Willow said they made it from roots and other tubers that grew in the area, as well as some leafy herbs and a mixture of venison.

"I'm curious to know what you meant by someone telling a lie caused Arthur's death," Connor said while everyone was enjoying the welcome change from hardtack and jerky for nooning.

"Oh, yeah," Will said, his head bobbing up and down on his long neck. "It all began before 1847, but the powder keg exploded, then, thanks t' Joe Lewis."

Willow nodded in agreement, her kind eyes once again growing sad.

"What began?" Landon asked.

"The Cayuse war," Will replied. "The reason why the Cayuse won't give a second thought t' killin' a white man if they can."

"Oh, my!" Louise Morland exclaimed. Her husband put his hand on her arm to calm her.

"Yes, ma'am, it ain't pretty. See, the Whitmans, Marcus and Narcissa, bless their souls, they came all the way out here, hopin' t' share their Christian faith and bring salvation to the lost folks out here in the wilderness. And they did good by them. Sure, there were a heap of misunderstandin's an' all, but they were good folks doin' what they figured t' be a good thing for the heathen."

Will paused to slurp up a spoonful of stew. He chewed slowly. Nobody said a word as they waited for him to continue.

"First it was the watermelons that one of their workers poisoned to stop the Cayuse takin' 'em off the land, but that wasn't the Whitmans' fault. Then there was the poisoned meat, meant for killin' the wolves," Will went on before being interrupted by Willow.

"Yes, and I tell my brothers, 'Don't eat that, it is bad medicine for the wolf,' but they do not listen, and so they become very, very sick." Her face was as earnest as her tone of voice.

"That's right," Will backed up her story. "Some of 'em already got mad at Whitman, that time, but he had warned 'em right early not t' eat that meat."

"So is that what started the war?" young Billy piped up, apparently eager to get to the climax of the story and echoing Gyorgyike's own unspoken question.

"Nah, it got worse than that. They got a measles outbreak, an' good ol' Whitman began takin' care of sick Cayuse. Put beds everywhere in his mission and treated 'em the best he could with what he had. Night an' day, he and Narcissa an' their workers, includin' my Willow here, was nursin' those sick Cayuse, but they were still dyin' like flies."

A murmur of pity and sorrow rose up collectively from the old mountain man's captivated audience.

"But they couldn't blame the poor Whitmans for the people dying, could they?" Lucy Morland asked in concern. "Surely the Cayuse could see they were doin' their best?"

Will shrugged. "Who knows?" he replied. "I know some of their own tried t' talk sense into the Cayuse who blamed the doctor instead of the disease."

"My people believe that if medicine man cannot save the life of one he treats, he must pay with his life," Willow interjected solemnly. "We who choose the way of the Lord Christ know this is not good thing to do."

"So that's where the feller tellin' a lie comes into it, right?" Connor conjectured.

"Sure does, sonny," Will said, nodding grimly. "Joe Lewis, half Iroquois, half white man, he took it into his head t' tell all the Cayuse that they were dyin' 'cause Whitman was poisonin' them, like he poisoned the wolves. Well, I figure that was all the Cayuse needed t' put them over the top, and they came roarin' down on that mission like a pack of wolves themselves one day. Left hardly a soul suckin' wind. My Willow, here, says God saved her life that day, an' I'm happy t' follow that reasonin'. Whoever or whatever it was saved her, brought her right to my cabin an' into my life, so I ain't complainin' none."

Will stopped, took a deep breath, and slurped up another spoonful of stew. The emigrants began murmuring among themselves. Gyorgyike sat silently, pondering the story she had just heard. These people who believed in God, they seemed to be putting the needs of others before their own most of the time. She looked over at Anna, who was listening intently to something Nellie was saying.

One after the other, memories rose up in Gyorgyike's mind of how Anna had shown her kindness and supported her in unexpected ways without being asked, and a restlessness began stirring in her heart. When the wagon train hit the trail once more, waving goodbye to Will and Willow, she decided she would take Anna aside, even if it had to be at the dead of night when nobody else was around, and ask her about her God who caused his followers to give their lives for others.

# Chapter 10
# The Dalles

Nooning times were usually peaceful, almost sleepy affairs, with occasional amiable banter exchanged while emigrants rested in the shade of their wagons or any available trees or watered their animals by whatever means were available. This day, however, there was a buzz around the communal fire pit. Even the children sat silently and listened, wide-eyed, while their elders debated the way forward.

After weeks of traveling the Blue Mountains, the emigrants approached a fork in the trail. To the north, if they kept on the trail that ran along the Columbia River, they would reach the Dalles, those churning, boiling rapids that had so many tales told about them since they had first set foot in Fort Hall. To the south ran the Barlow Road, as many called it, an alternative route that negated the need to face the dangers of the rushing waters of the Columbia. The four men of the alliance of families debated whether it would be a good choice to follow the widely proclaimed and acclaimed Barlow Road or take their chances on the river.

"Of course, I understand that the allure of a road that doesn't pose the dangers of the Dalles is naturally great," Clyde was saying, "but I think we would be remiss if we did not do due diligence and gather as much information as we can about this road and its unique dangers. I've not forgotten how narrowly we escaped taking a large gamble on the Applegate Cutoff."

"Ain't it just as big of a gamble takin' the river rapids?" Noel interjected, and Connor had to agree with him.

He had not forgotten that the trailblazers of the Applegate Cutoff had both lost children to the churning rapids. Even though Gabor was not his own son, he shuddered at the thought of the little boy being sucked to his death by the powerful whirlpools and undercurrents.

"It would be if we merely blundered in, going on only the word of a few advisors," Clyde agreed stoically. "Which is why I say we should do our due diligence before we decide upon either of the two, just as we did at Fort Hall."

"Clyde's right, I have t' say, fellers," Landon sided with his lieutenant. "We've seen how things can change over time, an' we've also seen how folks ain't always reliable in what they say. I say we wait till we get to the split in the trail tomorrow, then we camp there for a day or two and make sure we know everything we need t' know before we set our hearts on one thing."

Connor caught Noel's eye. "I'm thinking we should go along with the older folks," he said. "Much as I'm raring to go what seems the easier way, we know nothing about anything out here, and that's a fact."

Noel grinned wryly. "Now that you put it that way, all right. I'll be gatherin' information like my life depends on it."

"Actually, cowboy, it does," Landon said brusquely, but with a twinkle in his eye.

"Ha! Suckered again!" Noel exclaimed, slapping his thigh.

True to their word, the men spent their time at Fort Lee, the base of operations for the Emigrant Road at Dalles, gathering information on the two options that lay before them. They spent hours speaking to dragoons, officers, and fellow travelers, as well as the handful of locals who were gathering in the area. Connor felt a nagging in his gut to just pick the most obvious option and be on their way, but he held his impatience in check.

It wasn't easy. Gyorgyike was growing more distant, to where she barely spoke a word to him at all. Besides that troubling knowledge, he was tired. Tired of it all.

He wanted to be done with sleeping in a wagon on top of linen chests and food barrels. He wanted to sleep in a room with an ordinary bed and a roof overhead that did not leak. He wanted to be done with walking and riding and dragging lethargic oxen along the trail for the better part of every waking moment, one weary, aching step after the other.

In short, he wanted to have his life back again. Not even the breathtaking majesty of the surrounding scenery could lift his mood. His body, soul, and spirit were crying out for rest, for stillness and sanctuary. He sat with his hands folded and his head bowed as the others shared the information they had gleaned around the suppertime fires. The other three families were also in attendance for this important gathering.

"Seems ol' Sam Barlow gave up the toll road idea already," Noel was saying, his tone sober. "Folks kept usin' the trail, but it just got worse an' worse with nobody to take care of it."

"That's what I was told, too," Clyde agreed.

"Old man down at the Walla Walla village told me his people still use bits of the trail from time to time, an' they've seen folks havin' t' shoot their oxen from bein' injured, their wagons breakin' on the holes in the road. It ain't pretty," Landon added gravely.

"There're folks who reckon a feller'll lose more than what the toll cost by goin' that way now," Noel chimed in again.

"And it was a steep toll," Connor elaborated. "Five dollars a wagon at five different gates. Then we're not even talking about livestock. Some folks say one dollar, some say ten cents per head. I don't think any of us even have that much left."

"Turns out we don't really have a choice," Clyde said, his brow furrowed. "I spoke with some of the barge operators. It could take us some time before we have a barge booked to float our wagons down the river, and we'll have to send the women and children on foot along the clifftop with our animals."

"I bet the critters won't be sad they don't have to drag that old rattling wagon behind 'em anymore," Billy commented, despite it being the grown men's conversation.

"You're darn right, half-pint," Landon chuckled. "Still, it won't be easy. It's around ninety miles from here t' Fort Vancouver."

"That's another three weeks of walkin', if I ain't mistook," Noel noted dismally.

"You ain't mistook," Landon assured him unsympathetically. "Still, draggin' a wagon and tired oxen over mountain passes an' winchin' 'em down a hill like this," he tilted his arm into an angle greater than forty-five degrees, "could take a whole lot more out of a feller than hangin' onto his wagon an' raft down the whitewater. I reckon it'll be less strain on the womenfolk and the kids, too."

Connor felt suddenly grateful that Clyde's slow, ponderous nature had held them back from rushing into what had seemed, at first glance, to be a preferred choice. He couldn't imagine trying to winch the heavy wood and steel structure that had been his moving home for the last five months down a gradient of thirty degrees, let alone the fifty or sixty degrees that Landon had indicated.

"So we'll be moving out tomorrow, then, will we?" he asked, hoping the answer would be a resounding yes. He wanted to get the journey over with.

"I second that motion, Connor. All in favor, raise your right hand and say aye," Clyde announced solemnly. All the pioneers, women, and children raised their hands, and a chorus of ayes rose from the little group.

And so it was that, before the sun rose the following day, the party of seven wagons joined the queue that was forming around the launching place of the Columbia River section of the Emigrant Road. Bit by bit, they inched forward, and at last they were at the river's edge. The wide, smooth expanse of calmly flowing water belied the churning chaos that waited downstream.

"Let's be takin' them wheels off, mister," one of the barge operators remarked. "We'll be layin' that box flat on the raft, atop them wheels so we can be sure yer whole house don't go pitchin' into the water."

It was a laborious process. The wagon boxes needed to be emptied of their contents and the boxes themselves painted with pitch. Then the wheels were taken off and placed flat on the barge, which was nothing more than a large, rectangular raft built with young tree trunks lashed together. The wagon box was then lifted onto the raft by five or six men and its contents reloaded into it.

The women and children had prepared nooning rations and packed them in various containers like baskets and tin lunch boxes. These now swung from their shoulders. Some had slung filled water canteens, blankets, tents and other provisions across the backs of their livestock. They stood watching as the men securely lashed their wagons to the rafts and stepped aboard.

The brawny young man who was operating the Slades' barge gave Connor a white-toothed grin. His face was tanned brown by the sun, and his hands and arms bulged with sinew and muscle. "Here, mister, here's a pole for you t' work with," the young man said, handing Connor a long sapling trunk stripped of its branches and leaves. It was worn smooth at one end, while the other still sported bits of bark and was almost black from all the water it had absorbed from constant dipping in the river. "We'll use these t' push ourselves along and t' help balance when we hit the rapids. You ever done anything like this before, mister?"

"Can't say I have, Rick," Connor replied, dabbling in a vague childhood memory of a trip down a very gentle river on a much smaller raft.

"No matter," Rick proclaimed cheerfully. "Most folks haven't, but you'll catch on real quick, I promise."

With that, he hopped aboard the raft and began pushing the wooden contraption away from the bank. Some of the other rafts were already in the water, floating dreamily down the river in the midmorning sunshine. The light glistened on the water, and a cool breeze fanned Connor's face and arms.

He looked up toward the bank and saw the procession of women, children, and livestock already making their way along the beaten track carved out by many feet and hooves. The children were waving excitedly, and he waved back with his free hand. Their excitement was contagious, stirring a sense of anticipation in his chest.

This was it. The last leg of the journey. His gut twisted at the thought of what might await him when the barge reached the rapids, but a new flood of energy filled him when he remembered the end was in sight. Following the cues of his friendly barge operator, he helped guide the wagon down the river, leaving the women and children behind.

The barge operators had already informed them exactly how far they needed to go and where they would stop for the night. It felt good not to have to forge out the way themselves, but have directions. Connor's heart would have felt light as a feather if he didn't have the worry of what was to happen to himself and Gyorgyike once they reached Fort Vancouver.

He still felt the urge to finish what his grandfather had started and send the foreign powers packing back to Europe with their tails between their legs. Even though the provisional government had already been set up six years prior and Oregon was now fully a territory of the United States of America, there was still too much of a presence of non-Americans in the area for Connor's liking.

He did not know what Gyorgyike thought of that idea, though. Would she be happy with living in barracks? Would that be the final nail in the coffin of their already dead marriage? It had seemed like such a good idea to get a mail-order bride from Hungary, a beautiful one at that. Someone who was looking for adventure, as he was, someone who he could share the epic journey with, but the dream had burned out to ashes.

"Look lively, there, pardner!" Rick's voice broke in on Connor's musings, along with the sound of roaring waters growing louder in his ears by the second. The flow of the river had sped up, and the barge seemed to hurtle along at a rate of many knots.

The next few minutes felt like hours and yet went by in a flash of white foam, roaring waters, and the nauseating seesawing sensation of being thrust up into the air on the rushing waves, only to come crashing down as the waters tumbled away down into the rocks below. Using all his strength, Connor pushed his makeshift bargepole against the boulders to keep the raft from being dashed to pieces with the wagon and all.

As suddenly as they had appeared, the rapids gave way to a smooth stretch of river moving calmly along between the high cliff walls on either side. Drenched and exhausted, soaked from head to toe, and gasping great lungfuls of air, Connor jammed the pole between the logs of the crude river-craft and hung onto it, his legs feeling weak.

"You did good, mister," Rick complimented him with his habitual toothy grin.

Connor could only nod his rather doubtful acknowledgement.

And so the day wore on in much the same manner. For a while, the waters would be kind, flowing gently beneath the raft, and then, in an instant, it was as if a rabid, bloodthirsty water monster erupted beneath them, flinging the heavy raft and wagon about like a child's plaything.

By the afternoon, when the barge approached the first landing site where the party of emigrants would camp out for the night, Connor's whole body was aching. His hands felt bruised and stiff from clinging desperately to his barge pole and levering the raft out of harm's way more times than he could count.

One by one, the barges with their wagons perched on top drifted down the river and joined the others that had already landed. Just as the sun was shimmering golden on the gently undulating waters, the women and children came into view.

Dearbhla led the children in a rollicking Irish ditty, and even Gyorgyike seemed relaxed, but Connor felt as if he could sleep for a month of Sundays without waking up for anything.

"Look! Look!" Billy called out excitedly, holding up a string of limp, furry forms. "I shot us some rabbits for supper!"

Billy's bunnies, as they were affectionately called, went down very well for supper, and Connor slept like a log that night. The call to rise the next morning was especially difficult to obey, but he did so, and the previous day repeated itself, with just one difference: Connor was reading the dip and flow of the river and how to keep the raft from capsizing with a little less effort and stress. He noticed he was taking cues from his grinning barge captain and the journey became more tolerable, with some rapids worse than others.

At last, after eighteen seemingly endless days out on the river, they reached the end of the Dalles and could replace the wheels on their wagons. Connor had never thought he would be so happy to execute such a simple, meaningless task as in that moment.

He grinned up at Gyorgyike. "Only a couple of weeks and we'll be in our own little place," he said happily.

Gyorgyike blinked rapidly and looked away. "That will be wonderful, I'm sure," she said, her voice distant.

Connor paused in his work and straightened up. He wanted to say something, to demand an explanation from her for why she was treating him the way she was. As far as he could recall, he had done nothing to deserve the treatment she was giving him, and he wanted it to stop.

His hopes that she would thaw a little as they neared the end of the trail were clearly not happening. Still, he bit his tongue. Instead of railing against her, he sighed. "Wonderful, yeah."

That evening, as they rolled into Fort Vancouver, Connor made all haste to get his wagon and his family settled for the evening. Then he made his way to the officers' mess, where the dragoons were enjoying their evening meal.

A curious serviceman stopped him with a lopsided grin beneath his dapper military style mustache. "Say, you ain't one of us, are ya?" the man asked.

"No, but I'd like to be," Connor shot back, quick as a flash.

"You're sure about that?" the man teased, his brown eyes laughing.

"Sure as I'll ever be." Connor returned, grin for grin.

"Come with me," the man said and led him straight to the staff sergeant, a big, burly man with sandy hair clipped short and a clean-shaven face. His darting blue eyes assessed Connor from head to toe in an instant.

"Lookin' t' work the foreigners out of here, eh?" Staff Sergeant Finney remarked.

"Far as I'm concerned, they've got no business here, so they'd be better off leavin'," Connor confirmed the recruiter's suspicions.

"Well I reckon we can use you." Finney looked pleased. "How soon can ya step into line?"

"Tomorrow, if you want me to, but I just need to take care of some family business. I have a wife—"

"You shoulda told me that sooner, buddy," Finney interjected before Connor could elaborate. "Afraid there's no room for wives here. You can keep her in town and visit on weekends, but that's all we can offer ya. Go home and sleep on it with the missus, and you come tell me tomorrow, eh?"

Connor nodded and saluted awkwardly before beating a hasty exit.

That night when Gabor was asleep, he took his chance. "Gyorgyike, are you awake?"

"Yah, I am. What do you want?"

"I've joined the army here. You and Gabor can stay in town in Oregon City, and I'll only see you on weekends, but we could make it work." He stopped, waiting breathlessly for her response. It took a while to come, but when it did, it was cold and heartless.

"It does not matter what you do. I will leave to make my own home wit' just me and Gabor. I do not love you, Connor, and I will not lie to you anymore. When we go to Oregon City, I will get a claim for myself alone. I wish you well."

# Chapter 11
# End of the Road

The land claims office was a hive of activity. Clerks scurried back and forth between waiting emigrants and officials with large maps behind their desks full of black and white pins marking off parcels of land. Gyorgyike's heart was slowly sinking into her shoes at the words of the brisk and businesslike man behind the desk she sat at.

"I'm afraid, ma'am, according to the Donation Land Act of 1850, you cannot file a claim for three hundred and twenty acres, since you're not a man. The law clearly states single men are eligible to file claims and married men may claim an additional three hundred and twenty under the name of their wife."

"I was told that there are women who have done this," Gyorgyike stated, trying not to sound like she was begging and not feeling very successful.

"I'm afraid I can only go on what the law says, ma'am, not what people told you. I'm sorry if they misled you, but that is the way things stand here." The official looked sympathetic, but not willing to make any exceptions. Gyorgyike held her head high, even though her mind was racing as hard as her heart.

"Well, then I will have to see what else I can do," Gyorgyike said simply.

"I wish you all the best, ma'am," the official responded, sounding genuine. "I know there are employment opportunities available for a lady like you in the city. Maybe you'll find something there."

Gyorgyike nodded. "Thank you, sir," she said and took Gabor's hand. She got up and walked back to the place the families had agreed to meet once they were done filing their claims. She had come this far, and she had declared her independence to Connor. She could not possibly give up now. So many nights, she had dreamed of her patch of land with crops growing on it and sheep grazing in the meadow. It was too precious a dream to let go of just because she wasn't a man.

Anna and Clyde were the first to arrive at the agreed meeting place after Gyorgyike. "And how did it go?" Anna asked, excitement filling her voice.

Gyorgyike shook her head. "Not well, I am afraid. This official says I cannot file a claim because I am not a single man, but a single woman. He says I can find a job in the city, but that is not what I came here for." She paused. "But if there is no other way, I will have to do what he says and see if later I can get my piece of land that I have dreamed about for so long."

"What about the women we heard of who have filed claims?" Clyde asked, his voice and eyes showing deep concern.

"There is a new law, so I understand. The official said he is following the law and he can do nothing else. Only married women can file claims in their name through their husbands." Gyorgyike shrugged, not really wanting to speak about it at all.

"You and Connor are still married, though, right?" Anna said, a glimmer of hope in her eye.

Gyorgyike shook her head. "We are, but we will get the marriage annulled soon. I cannot pretend that we are married for this sake. It will be a lie."

"And what if you are reconciled?" Anna probed a little further.

Gyorgyike looked away. Connor had not said a word after she had told him of her intention to continue without him. He was at the army barracks now, probably being trained as a soldier and lustily living out his family heritage of freeing America from the colonists.

Looking back, she realized his patience and kindness had gone almost unnoticed by her in her bull-headed determination to become self-sufficient. She could not bring herself to admit it to anyone else, but she had been having doubts about her plan for a while. Doubts that she had repeatedly thrust from her mind. And yet she could not go back on what she had said simply because she was now in need.

"I think I have ruined any chance of that happening," she answered Anna's question sadly.

"I tell you what," Clyde said gently, placing a fatherly hand on Gyorgyike's shoulder. "You can set up house on our land until we can figure out a way to get you your own."

Gyorgyike stared at him disbelievingly. Had he just said what she thought he had said?

"Yes, I think that's a wonderful idea! Thank you, my love!" Anna exclaimed enthusiastically. Then she turned to look at Gyorgyike. "We'll have more than enough space for you as well. And I'm sure things will change sometime, somehow."

For a moment, Gyorgyike considered refusing their offer simply because she did not feel she deserved such kindness after the way she had treated Connor, but their beaming faces, eagerly awaiting her acceptance, compelled her to do exactly that. "That is very kind, Clyde and Anna. I promise I will work hard and do everything I can to get my land quickly," she said, wringing her hands in front of her.

"You'll never be a burden to us, if that's what you're thinking, Georgie," Anna replied gently. "And little Gabor and Fiona shouldn't have to be separated."

Gyorgyike nodded, feeling close to tears. It was a couple of days later that the real shock came, one that she would never have expected.

After purchasing a few spades and shovels, a plough and harness and a few other tools necessary for building their sod houses in time to beat the first winter snows, the emigrants headed for the Willamette Valley, minus Lorna Riley, the bachelors Greg Sawyer and Norman Hastings, and Henry Baker and his family. They had all elected to seek employment in and around Oregon City itself.

Gyorgyike walked beside the ox and the milk cow, drawing the wagon behind them for the very last time. She watched the settlers who had already been there for a season or more tending their crops and livestock while their children played outside or fished in the streams and rivers.

The autumn sun shone tenderly on the budding landscape, bathing everything in its glowing warmth. Birds called, insects buzzed, and the steady clip-clop of the draft animals' hooves took her closer and closer to her new home.

They had to travel almost a day upriver before the spaces between settled claims became large enough for the families to consider any of the empty claims. They had agreed they would all settle alongside each other to form a small community for support. At last, all agreed on a suitable spot near the swiftly flowing Willamette River.

The next day, the surveyor came out and staked their claims. Gyorgyike watched him from her wagon, the one Connor had left her with when he went to the army. It had not escaped her notice that Connor had not demanded payment of any kind for the wagon and livestock. She knew she would have to travel up to Fort Vancouver sometime or another to get the marriage annulled, but she was not sure if she could face him yet.

Once more, she wondered if she had indeed made the right decision to follow her own path without Connor. It had been easy to see him as merely a pawn in her game of chess against life at the beginning, but all his kindnesses were stacking up against her and her intentional deceit. She hardly noticed what was going on around her while she battled the guilt assuaging her soul.

"Here you are, ma'am," a deep male voice droned, startling her from her inner struggles. "Your land claim invoice." A tall, black-bearded man stood before her, holding out a long slip of paper with writing, a stamp, and a signature on it.

"Land claim invoice?" Gyorgyike repeated uncomprehendingly.

"Yes, ma'am, for you and your husband, Connor Slade. You are Mrs. Connor Slade, are you not?"

Gyorgyike blinked. "Ah, yes. I am, but…" She broke off as Anna and Clyde stepped closer.

"That's right, Mr. Jones," Clyde said in his decisive voice that didn't invite argument. "This is Mrs. Connor Slade, and she'll be taking care of their claim while Mr. Slade is serving in the army up at Fort Vancouver."

"Sure. That's what the recorder said," the surveyor responded, still holding out the slip of paper to Gyorgyike.

She took it with trembling fingers, unable to believe her ears. In an act of complete selflessness, Connor had filed a claim for the two of them, knowing she did not want him around. She felt her face grow hot with shame.

"Well a good day to you, folks," the surveyor said, stepping back and doffing his hat to them. "I wish you every success on your new land."

The moment felt surreal, and Gyorgyike wished Connor was there to share it with her. She swallowed down the lump in her throat and folded the paper in two, carefully stowing it in the box where she kept important things.

"Well, folks! Let's get settled on our land!" Noel announced with a whoop.

"First thing to do is build those sod houses," Landon declared briskly. "Noel, I reckon Jasper is about the strongest critter we have. Would ya mind if we used him for cuttin' the sod?"

"I was about to suggest it," Noel replied, going to fetch the big horse where he was picketed.

An air of festivity filled the atmosphere around the little group as Noel led Jasper up and down, drawing the plow behind him and overturning the rich, black turf, while the others took turns with the spades, cutting the sod into even, rectangular blocks. Next, a patch of land had to be cleared for the sod walls to be built around. Excitedly, the emigrants picked the best spots for their houses and went to work, each family building their new home layer by layer.

"We'll do your house tomorrow, Gyorgyike," Clyde assured her. "Why don't you go pick out the spot you'd like to build it in? I'll get Matt to clear it for you."

"I think that is a wonderful idea, Clyde, thank you," Gyorgyike said gratefully, making her way over to the plot of land just over half a mile in length and breadth that was now hers. She chose a spot as far away from the others as she could without going right to the edge of the property. Not because she didn't want to be near them. It was just that she wanted—no, needed—all the solitude she could get. At least for a while.

Nobody seemed to notice this little detail when she pointed out her chosen patch of land for her sod house. As the walls rose higher and higher, the women worked together to trim the angular bits hanging out and the excess grass so that the surface became smoother and more like an actual wall. The sloping roof was made with poles from the few cedar and fir trees dotted about the area. They covered the poles with dried brush and more sod and clay.

Clyde, the group's resident carpenter, happily fashioned windows, and a door from the wood of the wagon that had carried Gyorgyike and Gabor and Connor all the way over the dusty plains and soaring mountains. It seemed only fitting that it should be used to build her first small house. Clyde also built two cots for Gyorgyike and Gabor to sleep on.

With all the barrels and chests of provisions inside, Gyorgyike set about making her house feel like home. Removing the musty but still serviceable sheets, tablecloths, pillows, and blankets from the chest that had belonged to Connor's mother, Gyorgyike felt a pang of guilt again. She wondered if Connor was happy serving in the army, honoring his grandfather's memory.

***

Two weeks had passed since Connor had made his way back to the staff sergeant's office at Fort Vancouver and signed up for training. It had been a grueling two weeks, in some ways similar and in some ways completely different from the hardships he had faced to get to Oregon.

The early morning drills were simply child's play. He had been woken every morning by sparrows for the last six months. The fitness training was a breeze. It had pushed him to the limits of human endurance, crossing rivers and mountain passes on almost a daily basis. The food was awful. Nothing could be worse than hardtack and nearly rancid jerky on an empty stomach.

What was more difficult to get used to was the human element. The fort had been set up alongside the Hudson's Bay Company premises when the US government had sent their troops to Oregon after the 1846 provisional government of Oregon was formed. Over time, the US Army had taken over more and more of the HBC's land and buildings. It was a slow but inexorable process of removing the colonist element.

"We're pullin' out the weeds, little by little," one infantryman told him with deep satisfaction. "Soon they'll all be gone, and Oregon will be ours."

Connor had thought these kinds of words would cheer him, but it was becoming clear to him that battling imagined enemies in his head was a far cry from looking into the eyes of men very much like himself and telling them they had less of a right to be here than he did.

The turning point came one day when he was working in the fort's vegetable garden. It was his turn, ironically enough, to do the weeding, along with two other army recruits. The sun beat down, and the air was sultry, despite the fact fall had already turned the leaves of the cottonwoods brilliant yellow. An unsuspecting HBC employee wandered closer, looking for ripe pumpkins in a pumpkin patch.

Connor hardly noticed the man. His thoughts were on Gyorgyike, wondering whether she was happy following her dream of independence and if little Gabor was still chattering away to Fiona only, or perhaps had talked to others in the group as well.

"Hey!" one man called.

The HBC employee, noticeable by the lack of uniform, looked up and walked away as fast as he could, but it was not fast enough. The two recruits caught up with him and brought him roughly to a standstill.

"He's got time for scratchin' around in the pumpkin patch. You figure he's got time for doin' our weedin' for us?" one of them sneered to the other.

"Sure, he has. What have them HBCs got to do here, anyway? We're in charge here, now. We're runnin' the show," his friend returned gleefully.

The HBC employee didn't respond at all. He just kept shifting his little round eyeglasses up higher on the bridge of his nose and blinking rapidly as he stared at his feet. The two recruits each grabbed an arm, and all but dragged the tripping, stumbling man to their hoes.

"Here," the first recruit said, shoving a hoe handle into the man's shaking hand. "Clear out all 'em weeds and be quick about it."

The other recruit suddenly seemed to notice Connor, who was still hacking away at the weeds in his row with his head down. "Hey, Slade! What you still hoein' for? We got us a colonizer here can do the work for us. Come catch forty winks with us," he said.

Connor took a deep breath. He had been ignoring much of what was being done to the employees of the HBC, feeling, in some part, that they were getting their just desserts, and he still didn't want to be drawn into anything, but a sense of regret and injustice was taking hold of him. He planted the end of his hoe on the ground and leaned on it, peering intently at the men opposite him. "I'm not too lazy to hoe my row," he drawled. "And I'm sure this gent has his own work to do, don't you, sir?" He turned his focus on the small man now standing with the hoe in his hand.

"I suppose so," the man stammered, "although I really don't mind—"

"There we go. You heard the man," Connor interrupted him as he addressed his two fellow recruits. "He's got his own work to do, so we may as well leave him be. I'm sure if he had time, he'd help us."

The man nodded vigorously.

"Whose side you on, Slade?" the first recruit snarled threateningly.

"Whose side?" Connor repeated, tilting his head to one side to show he was seriously pondering the recruit's question. "I don't reckon it's a matter of whose side I'm on, but what I'm standing for. I've just come across two thousand miles of the most difficult country I've ever seen, and I've seen the measure of a man is not where he comes from or what he sounds like. It's about whether he has respect for others as well as himself. In fact, I reckon respecting others is a sure sign a man respects himself."

He hadn't planned to say all that. He hadn't even pondered it before that moment. It was as if everything he had seen already and every gut reaction he had felt toward the things he saw had somehow changed him inwardly without him even knowing it was happening.

The two recruits stared at him, their lips twitching as they seemed to be casting about for some smart remark to make.

"Here, we can work together," Connor said to the Englishman without thinking. He gave the men who were holding onto him a pointed stare, and they released their prisoner.

Without missing a beat, the man walked over to Connor, held out his hand, and said, "It's a pleasure to meet you, Mr. Slade. I'm George Caldwell."

# Chapter 12
# Miracles

"Well, George Caldwell, you can call me Connor." He took the Englishman's hand of friendship and found his own arm being pumped ecstatically up and down. "You can also go back to your office if you like, or whatever it is you need to do."

"They asked me to take some pumpkins to the kitchen," George explained. "But I can help you, if you'd like."

"How about you help me with these weeds, and I'll help you with your pumpkins?" Connor suggested. "I really have little more to do."

"I think that's a capital idea," George responded.

Connor studiously kept his focus on his new friend, but he could see the disgruntled recruits out of the corner of his eye hacking away furiously at their rows of carrots.

"That was a very kind thing you did, you know?" George said as he pulled out a handful of weeds and tossed them into the wheelbarrow that Connor had standing nearby. "I'm curious to know what made you do it. I'm not used to American soldiers treating me kindly."

"Yeah," Connor admitted, chopping out some weeds with the edge of the hoe. "It's something I've noticed, too. Truth be told, I came here to do exactly what they were just doing.

I wanted to chase all the colonizers out of Oregon and back to England or France or wherever it is they belong."

George chuckled dryly. "I can't say I blame you, Yankee," he quipped. "There were a lot of British officers and HBC bigwigs who made life a living hell for the American settlers and businessmen before 1846 rolled around. I suppose we Britons are simply reaping what we sowed, if we're honest."

Connor paused in his hoeing. "That's something I never expected to hear a Briton say, myself," he stated with a wry smile.

"Well, hopefully I won't be one for long," George countered with his own lopsided grin. "I met a lovely Wishram woman, White Bird, and I'm hoping to marry her. Of course, that means I'll have to be naturalized, you know? And who wouldn't want to be? I'd only lived here a month before I fell in love with the place. Can't imagine going back to Oxford, even if it is my birthplace."

Connor stared at him. "You're thinking of becoming an American?" he asked. "So basically, you're defecting?"

George laughed. "I suppose you could put it that way," he replied. "Just like the Father of Oregon, as some people like to call him. Our very own French-Canadian, John McLoughlin. He's the one who put Fort Vancouver and Oregon City on the map, and everybody loves him, except those who would rather see Yankees hang from a yardarm."

"I don't know why I didn't think of this before," Connor said, repenting wholeheartedly of his former hatred. "My grandfather was a Briton who defected from the British navy during the War of Independence. Why wouldn't there be men today who do the same thing?"

"Your grandfather, eh?" George sounded impressed. "Well, it really doesn't come as much of a surprise to me. You'd naturally want to defend the land he defended, and truly, this land has a way of making one want to fight to keep it free."

Connor smiled. "It does, doesn't it?" he agreed.

The two completed the weeding of Connor's row of carrots, and then he made good on his promise to help George pick some suitable pumpkins for the HBC headquarters' kitchen. They walked in silence, each one consumed with his own thoughts. Connor's were drifting back to the Hendersons and Morlands and Tanners. And Gyorgyike.

There had not been a day when he had not wondered about her, but he had adamantly pushed the thought of her and Gabor from his mind. He had a purpose in being in the army, a purpose that would help shape the future of the state of Oregon, once it was named that. At least, that was what he had believed.

All at once, he felt as if he was in limbo. The driving force that had brought him to the barracks beside the Columbia River was quickly on the wane, and he wondered if that really was where his future lay. He had a homestead waiting to be built and a wife he could at least try to convince to stay with him.

He sighed. Then again, the chances of that being successful were slimmer than a hair's breadth.

"Penny for your thoughts," George quipped, giving Connor a sidelong glance.

"Not sure they're worth a penny," Connor replied dryly. "But I guess since you shared yours…" He trailed off. "I'm uncertain I'm meant to be here anymore. I figured I was honoring my grandfather's legacy, but now I'm having my doubts. And I've a wife and stepson who need me down in Willamette Valley. Only trouble is she doesn't want me. Does that make any sense at all?"

"Sense?" George repeated. "When did life ever make sense? You should get back down there as soon as you can. Whatever there was can be saved. You believe that, Connor." George's eyes were bright with hope and anticipation.

Connor wished he could share the man's optimism, but even as the thought crossed his mind, he felt the infectious effects of his new friend's lust for life. "It won't be easy. I think I've ruined all my chances with her, and I'm not even sure how I did that. But I can't stay here, and she's living on a claim that is half mine, anyhow."

"You've got this sewn up so tight, it's a cinch!" George declared, grinning from ear to ear. "You'd better make sure you come look me up if you ever need to come to Oregon City. I'd love to hear how things go for you."

They had reached the kitchen by that juncture and placed the fat, round, bright orange pumpkins on the large table in the center.

"I didn't plan on it this morning, but I reckon right about now's the time I'll be going down to the staff sergeant's office and handing in my resignation," Connor stated as he dusted his hands off on his standard issue army trousers.

"Best decision you'll ever make," George said. "I wish you all the best, Connor. Go out there and take the bull by the horns!"

The two men shook hands warmly, and then Connor turned and left, striding down the gravel road that lay between the HBC headquarters building and the US Army barracks. The staff sergeant didn't seem too surprised by his announcement that he was resigning from the corps. He quickly drafted a letter, which Connor signed, and then sent him on his way.

"I figured you wouldn't be around too long," he remarked. "Those miles on the Emigrant Road do things to folks. They just think different once they get here."

Connor didn't waste time pondering what the staff sergeant meant. Instead, he hurried back to his bed in the barracks, shoved the few possessions he had into an army-issue knapsack, saddled his horse, and rode away from the military camp, southward toward Willamette Valley.

He did not know where his wagon train friends had settled, but he would just have to keep riding and ask people along the way. It had been two weeks already, and folks must surely know something about new settlers in the area. From what Clyde had told him, they would look higher up the river, toward the southern end of the valley, rather than close to Oregon City. That would help a little at least to give him direction.

It was already midafternoon, and he had little time before dark. He urged the horse on along the trail, scanning the valley floor and the surrounding hills for anything or anyone familiar, even though he knew it would be a few hours before he would come near the place where his friends had settled.

Even as he searched, he imagined what he would say to Gyorgyike. *I know you don't want me around, but I can't just leave you to build up a homestead on your own.* No, she wasn't on her own, really. The Hendersons and Morlands would make sure of that. They had become like family to both of them along the trail, of that there was no doubt.

*I know you don't want me around, but maybe we could just share the land, and that way you could still have your dream. That's all I want, really.* It was a lie. It wasn't all he wanted. He wanted her to love him the way he loved her. His time alone at Fort Vancouver had proven to him he enjoyed living with Gyorgyike, even with her withdrawn, unresponsive ways. He knew her simply by watching her interact with others, and there seemed to be a genuineness in her that few others possessed.

*I missed you more than I thought I would and...* That just sounded cheesy. Although it was disconcertingly close to the truth.

*God, if you're there, I could use a little help on this,* he thought fleetingly and focused his attention once more on the countryside and the settlements that were filling it.

***

Gyorgyike sat on her cot by the stove, soaking up its warmth. She looked down at Gabor and smiled. He was sitting on the rug in front of the oven, telling himself a story, dramatized with some carved wooden animals Connor had made for him while they were still on the trail. His childish mutterings were the sweetest thing Gyorgyike had ever heard. Not merely because they were the innocent ramblings of a child, but because he had been silent for so long.

She remembered how Connor had told her about Gabor talking to Fiona. She had not believed him at first, thought it was just a ploy to get her to interact with him, but he had been right. Gabor was now speaking to her, too. Every day he added words to his vocabulary and tried them out on his mother. Gyorgyike helped him say some words correctly, but she worried he would pick up her accent.

A log crackled in the fire box of the tiny oven. The house felt suddenly too empty, and she missed Connor's sturdy, dependable presence for the hundredth time that week. It was as if he were haunting her, and she could not escape his memory. Six months on the trail had evidently cemented some sort of bond between them, despite her efforts to prevent anything like that from happening.

She sighed and lay down on the cot. It had surprised her how warm the sod house was during the night and how cool it seemed when the day temperatures reached their peak. She gazed up at the sheet Anna had helped her hang beneath the rafters to keep the dust and soil from the sod roof from falling into her food or hair.

It was a strange little house, but it was home. Her home. Nobody told her what to do and when to do it. There were no more endless miles of walking to be completed every day. She had a relatively comfortable place to sleep with a hay tick that was far softer than the wooden chests and barrels covered with a lumpy horsehair mattress that had been her bed for six long months.

She was alone with her thoughts. That had seemed like something to look forward to, but the longer she thought, the more those thoughts seemed to overwhelm her. With no distractions around her, the awful truth of her past and what they had done to her rose like a sea monster out of the depths of her mind and blotted out the light.

Night after night, she woke up crying out, her cheeks wet with tears from the nightmares that plagued her. Instead of feeling free from the embrace of another human being, she longed to have strong, comforting arms around her.

Later that night, two weeks after she had moved from the wagon to the soddie, she lay in her cot, trying to calm her breathing after waking from yet another nightmare. All at once, a realization struck her. She had had no nightmares out on the trail, and looking back, she knew why. Connor's mere presence beneath the wagon and, later, behind her in the wagon, had made her feel secure. Unlike all the other men in her life that she could remember, he had not posed a threat but had been a haven of safety.

Hot tears stung her eyes once more. This time not out of fear but deep, sorrowful regret. The surrounding people, including Connor, had constantly reached out to her and still did. And yet she had consistently kept them at bay, fearful to let anyone close to her heart. She knew it was wrong, but she felt helpless to change her response toward them. Then Anna's kindly, peaceful face rose up before her mind's eye.

*Anna's God,* she prayed without intending to. *I think I need you. I think I cannot carry on like this, with all the pain and fear and hatred in my heart. I don't know what to do with it. Please, if you can, and if you want to, please help me!*

Her thoughts were barely cold when the sound of rapid hoof beats came pounding through the still night air. Drunken voices yelled something unintelligible, and at the next moment, hard fists were hammering on her door. Gyorgyike's heart began racing so hard it hurt as she sat up and wrapped herself in the quilt. Three male voices demanded to be let in, their demands peppered with crude remarks and coarse laughter.

Gyorgyike froze with fear while her panicked mind raced in search of a solution to her dilemma. She could scream, but there was little chance anyone would hear her. The nearest house to hers was Anna and Clyde's house, and they were over two miles away.

She could try to run, but there was no way she could outrun three powerful men. And she could not leave Gabor behind. It soon became clear that even if she decided what to do, it would come too late. The sound of splintering wood filled the soddie, and Gabor cried out, "Mama!" His little voice was filled with fear and alarm.

"Hide behind the stove, Gabor!" she instructed him in Hungarian, and in the darkness, she saw his shadow moving toward the place she had indicated.

With a crash, the door fell inward into the house, and three pairs of boots trampled over it. Pale moonlight streamed in at the doorway, silhouetting the bulky intruders. Gyorgyike screamed, but a rough hand clamped over her mouth and muffled it.

"Don't fight us, sweetheart, it ain't no use. This'll be over before ya know it," a gruff voice laden with the stench of stale whiskey growled into her ear.

Gyorgyike clamped her teeth down hard on the hand that covered her lips. The steely taste of blood filled her mouth, but she didn't care. A deafening roar erupted beside her head, and something hard hit her jaw. She began clawing and kicking at the arms that were trying to pin her down on the floor, screaming at the top of her lungs and biting every time a hand tried to silence her.

She knew they would overpower her, but she refused to stop fighting. She refused to let them have their way. Even if it killed her. "God! Anna's God! Help me! Please, help me!" she cried out, not wanting to die, not wanting to leave little Gabor without a mother or father in the world.

Suddenly, the sound of a rifle shot thundered through the air and reverberated in the tiny house, making her ears ring. Through a mist of shock, Gyorgyike wondered if the men had shot her, but she could not tell by any form of physical pain since her whole body was aching. The hands gripping her arms and legs slacked off, as if distracted.

"If you stinking yellow-bellied coyotes don't want to wind up dead, you'd best leave my wife alone!" a man's furious voice boomed through the air.

*Connor?* Gyorgyike could hardly believe her ears. Was she dreaming? Had she hit her head and now imagining things? But there was no mistaking the fact that she was free. No cruel hands restrained her; no nauseating odor of old alcohol filled her nostrils. The sound of scrambling boots was followed by the rapid patter of horse hooves fading into the distance.

The rifle boomed again for good measure. Then Connor was beside her, kneeling in the moonlight. "Georgie, are you all right? Did they hurt you? I'm so sorry I didn't come sooner. I'm so sorry, Georgie, please forgive me." His voice cracked with guilt and worry, but he didn't touch her.

Staring up at his face shrouded in shadow, Gyorgyike felt her heart break. He had come back, for no reason, and exactly when she needed him. He had appeared right after she had cried out to Anna's God to save her. It was a miracle in so many ways. A miracle she didn't deserve. Tears began rolling down her cheeks as she felt Gabor's thin, little arms wrap around her neck. "How did you know?" she asked Connor, already knowing the answer.

"I didn't," he replied. "I just knew I had to come home tonight."

"It *is* a miracle," Gyorgyike choked out before she crawled into his arms and bawled like a baby for the first time in her adult life.

# Chapter 13
# Green Pastures

Connor held his wife's shaking form, still reeling from the shock of finding three men assaulting her in the little sod house. He had prepared himself for a completely different scenario: an aloof and defiant Gyorgyike refusing to even hear what he had to say, let alone speak to him.

The burning anger he had felt coursing through his veins at the sight of her being attacked had been just as unexpected. He had come so close to pointing the rifle at the man's back, but at the last moment, he lifted the barrel and fired into the sod wall of the house.

His hands shook as much as his insides as he sat on the hard-packed earth floor and rocked Gyorgyike back and forth in silence.

Gabor stroked her arm, saying, "Don't cry, Mama, don't cry."

At last, his mother's sobs lessened, and she drew away from Connor, wiping her eyes with the hem of her nightdress. Without a word, she got up and went to light a lantern. Turning to face him, she smiled a broken smile. "Thank you, Connor, for saving me and Gabor from those horrible men," she said and sat down on the cot behind her, looking crumpled and fragile.

Connor stood to his feet and hesitated. "May I sit down there?" he asked, pointing at the edge of the cot beside her.

Gyorgyike nodded and patted the open space.

Connor sat down carefully, making sure not to touch her unless she made a move toward him.

"I have not treated you right, Connor Slade," Gyorgyike said, staring at her bare feet on the floor. "I do not know why you would come back to me at all, but you are here and now I want to tell you everything. I think I owe you this, no?"

"You don't owe me a darn thing, Georgie," Connor protested vehemently. "I should never have left you alone and gone off to do my own thing. I should have just stuck around here with the rest of the wagon train. This would never have happened to you if I'd been around to begin with."

"You are forgetting it was me who chased you away, Connor," Gyorgyike countered, her eyes filling with fresh tears as she looked earnestly into his face. "And it was never your fault. You did not deserve that. It was me, and the things that have happened to me since I was a little girl."

She turned her eyes back to the floor and took a ragged breath, releasing it with a shaky sigh. Connor sat silently and listened as she told him, in halting, tearful words, of the things she had lived through since the tender age of twelve. He could hardly believe what his ears were hearing. Hot and cold waves of alternating anger, horror, sorrow, and pity washed over him while he listened.

But most of all, a sense of deep understanding filled him. The mystery that had been Gyorgyike no longer evaded him. Her cold, indifferent distance. Her resistance to his touch, even a hand on her arm or an arm around her shoulders. Her desire to be independent. It all made sense now.

At last, she was done, and it soaked the hem of her nightdress in tears. Connor sat in silence beside her for a while, unsure of what to do next. Gyorgyike sighed again and shifted closer to him, then laid her head against his shoulder. He reached up and stroked her hair.

"As long as there is breath in my lungs, nobody will ever harm you or Gabor again," he said gruffly, tears pricking his eyes.

His wife slipped her arms around his waist and hugged him close. "Thank you, Connor," she whispered hoarsely.

A movement caught Connor's eye, and he looked down to see Gabor clambering to his feet. The little boy's soulful black eyes were locked on Connor's in a gaze that spoke of greater understanding than his young years warranted. He climbed up onto Connor's lap, wrapped his arms around his neck with a hug as tight as his mother's. "Thank you, Papa," he said simply, and Connor broke down at last.

***

Gyorgyike woke to the usual dawn chorus and the sun peeking through the gap in her curtains. Everything was the same as it had been the day before, but everything was different. She was not alone. She opened her eyes to see Connor just pulling his suspenders up over his shoulders.

Gyorgyike sat up in her cot. "Why did you not wake me?" she asked sleepily. "I could have made breakfast already."

"You aren't doing a thing today if I have any say about it," Connor told her. "Not until we're sure you're not badly hurt. How do you feel this morning?"

Gyorgyike moved her limbs a little, cautiously flexing and stretching them, alert to any extreme pain. Mostly, there was just a dull ache. Only her jaw felt very sensitive. She stroked it gingerly with her fingertips. "I think this is where one of them punched me," she said.

Connor stepped closer, his eyes dark with anger and worry. He peered at her jawline. "Hmmm... It's purple and blue and quite swollen. You sure that's all that's hurting?"

"Well, no, my whole body feels like a wagon ran it over," Gyorgyike admitted, sitting up and looking around the one-roomed house. "Where is Gabor?"

"He's outside, playing in the dirt. Said he wants to make mud pies for you for breakfast," Connor told her.

"He spoke to you?"

"Sure did," Connor said, beaming.

Gyorgyike lay back on the cot and pulled the blanket up over her. "I cannot lie here all day, but I wish I could."

"Of course you can," Connor countered. "In fact, if I find you outside that cot today, I'll send you right back."

"But there is so much work to do," Gyorgyike protested.

"Georgie, I'm begging you. Stay right where you are and let me take care of you. I'll be riding over to the Hendersons in a bit, soon as we've had breakfast."

Gyorgyike turned to look at the stove. There was a pot of oatmeal bubbling away on top of it. It felt good to be looked after. She turned back to Connor. "All right, you win. I will stay in bed today and sleep as much as I can. But if I feel better, may I get up and do something small at least?"

"I'll think about it," Connor replied, giving her a lopsided grin that made her heart leap.

After the three of them had eaten their simple breakfast, Connor made good on his word and went over to the Hendersons to let them know what had happened and that he was back for good. A little flurry of fear flitted around in Gyorgyike's gut as she watched his departing back through the window. She beat it down adamantly. He would not stay away long. He had seen what leaving her alone exposed her to.

Less than an hour later, Connor returned with Anna and Nellie in tow. They fussed over her and took care of Gabor and his needs, as well as regularly giving Gyorgyike smelling salts and replacing the cool, wet cloth on her forehead. Anna made a poultice for her bruised jaw and chamomile tea for her jangled nerves.

Later in the day, Fiona came to play, and Clyde even stopped by to cheer her up with a selection of beautiful and happy tunes on his violin. Louise arrived with some sweet biscuits, and Carrie produced an enormous bouquet of white and yellow wildflowers.

"They're goldenrod and bunchberry flowers," Carrie told her. "Yellow always makes me feel happy. I hope it will do the same for you, Georgie."

"I am feeling so happy already," Gyorgyike replied, trying not to get too emotional. "Just having you all come to help and comfort me is making me happier than I have ever been."

By the next day, the aches and pains had faded to a slight stiffness, and she rose early to bake scones and fry eggs and bacon for a proper breakfast. As the little family sat together, eating their morning meal, and watching the sun rise over the Cascade Mountains, Gyorgyike reached out and placed her hand over Connor's. He jumped slightly and swallowed the mouthful of food he had been chewing before looking at her expectantly.

"I wish to go speak wit' Anna today," Gyorgyike said solemnly.

"All right," Connor readily agreed. "Mind if I ask what you wish to speak about with her?"

"I prayed to her God to help me twice on the night you came here, and he has done it. I want to know more about him."

Connor stared at her silently for a few moments. Then he cleared his throat. "I prayed to him, too. On the ride out here," he said, looking a little embarrassed. "I also prayed that he would help me."

"And did he?" Gyorgyike enquired eagerly.

Connor nodded. "He did," he said, still looking sheepish.

"He helped you to find me?" she probed further, wondering about his strange response.

"I suppose you could put it like that," Connor said, and cleared his throat.

Gyorgyike stared at him uncomprehendingly.

Connor shifted uncomfortably on his makeshift stool. "I came back to make you my wife properly, Gyorgyike," he said. "I didn't know how I was going to do it. I rehearsed many things to say to you, but I didn't use any of them."

Gyorgyike's heart leaped. "I know. You told me you were sorry, and I did not know why because you were not the one who was needing to apologize for anything." She smiled. "I am glad he helped you, too."

"So am I," Connor assured her.

A moment of silence hung between them. Except for the sound of Gabor humming a nursery rhyme that Fiona had taught him, they finished their meal in silence.

"So, I guess we both want to know more about Anna's God," Connor said at last. Wiping his mouth on his sleeve.

"Stop doing that," Gyorgyike told him. "We are no longer living on the trail."

Connor looked confused, and Gyorgyike pointed to his sleeve. He laughed. "Come on, let's go to the Hendersons' place."

As they approached their neighbor's yard, Billy came running toward them. "Have you come to visit? Oh, this is so much fun, living in an actual house again and having neighbors!"

"We sure have, half-pint," Connor replied laughingly. "Is your ma busy? We'd like to speak with her."

"I don't know if she's busy, but she is inside. I'm pretty sure she'll stop whatever she's doin' to talk to y'all."

Billy led the way to the sod house. It was a little bigger than Gyorgyike and Connor's, but Gyorgyike felt sure they still crowded it with the whole family inside. It was no wonder most of the family members were already out and about, even in the chilly fall morning.

"Georgie! Connor! How lovely to see you," Anna welcomed them in, and Billy scampered off, taking Gabor with him. "Are you feeling better, Georgie? That bruise of yours surely looks much less angry than it did yesterday."

"I am feeling much better, thank you, Anna," Gyorgyike replied gratefully. "It is the kindness of this group of people that has made me better. But there is something else we would like to speak wit' you about."

"All right," Anna agreed, "whatever I can do to help, I'll do." She poured tea for all three of them and handed out the steaming cups.

Gyorgyike took a sip of tea. "Can you tell us more about your God?" she asked simply, feeling as if there were grander words needed but not knowing how else to phrase the simple desire in her heart.

Anna's eyes misted up with tears, but she was smiling, so Gyorgyike deduced they must be tears of joy. "It would be my greatest pleasure to share everything I know about him," she said, clasping her hands in her lap. "I would like to ask one question first, though. May I know what prompted you to ask me this?"

Gyorgyike looked at Connor. He nodded. Briefly, Gyorgyike outlined the story of her and Connor's answered prayers.

"We have heard of you praying to your God on the trail and seen him answer you, and we have seen how kind you are," she concluded. "But now we have prayed to your God ourself, and he has answered us, too. Even if we do not know him, he answers us. I am thinking it can only be good to know such a God who answers people like us, who are not good people like you."

While she listened, Anna covered her mouth with her hand. Her eyes grew wide. As soon as Gyorgyike was done, she threw her hands in the air. "Oh! I don't quite know what to say!" she exclaimed, tears brimming in her eyes. "Except that I am not good. Not at all. I have many faults, but it is because of my faults that I can glory in the cross alone. Only God is good. And yes, he is so good he answers the prayers of sinners, including me."

Gyorgyike caught Connor's eye again. He shrugged. "I do not understand?" Gyorgyike said questioningly to Anna. "How do you mean, 'glory in the cross'? What cross is this, and why do you glory in it?"

"I'm sorry," Anna blustered. "I'm a little taken aback by your request, I suppose, because I wasn't expecting it. Let me begin at the beginning."

She told them the story of salvation. It was a story Gyorgyike had never heard before. A story that filled her with wonder and awe. A story that was more than just a story. She knew it was true in the depths of her soul. While Anna was speaking, Clyde entered the sod house and sat down quietly beside his wife. Gyorgyike could tell he was listening, too.

"Now, this invitation is open to you, too, just as it was to me and all who have accepted it," Anna concluded. "If you are sure you want to surrender your lives to the lordship of Christ, I can lead you in a prayer to do that."

"Wait," Clyde cut in, his hand on his wife's shoulder. "I need to call the children. They need to hear this."

Anna looked surprised. "I've told them about God before," she said hesitantly. "And I've prayed with them, too."

"Not like this, you haven't," Clyde replied, his eyes bright with intensity. "They need to hear this," he repeated.

"All right," Anna agreed meekly. "I'll wait."

She kept busy, putting on another pot of tea while Clyde went to fetch their brood of children. Curiosity rampant on their faces, they filed into the little house, and it turned out to be just as cramped as Gyorgyike had expected.

Once more, Anna told the story. Gyorgyike found she didn't mind listening to it a second time. In fact, she would have welcomed a third and even a fourth telling. At last, the time came for the prayer to be said.

"You must all remember, this is not something to be done lightly. You must only pray this prayer if you are willing to lay down you own will and your own plans for your life. God doesn't play second fiddle to anyone."

Gyorgyike nodded. She knew she was ready. Everything she had done to regulate her own life had failed. Everything she had done to be a good person had failed. She was tired of carrying the hatred and bitterness in her heart. Tired of trying to be strong. Tired of feeling guilty.

As she repeated the words Anna spoke, she felt herself relinquishing everything she held onto from her past. She had the sensation of getting lighter and lighter until she felt sure she would go floating away if she didn't hang onto something heavy.

Echoing Anna's final amen, Gyorgyike looked up. She felt different. Everything else looked different, too. The very room seemed brighter. All the colors she had hardly noticed before now jumped out at her and demanded her attention. She looked at Connor. He looked different, too. She tried to find out what had changed. She looked over at Clyde. The big man had tears glistening in his eyes. Then she realized.

The hatred was gone. The bitterness was gone. The fear was gone. The distrust was gone. In its place was peace, contentment, and a vibrant joy bubbling up in her soul. She laughed and gripped Connor's hand.

Then she remembered something and grew sober. "Connor, I never apologized for not telling you about Gabor," she whispered. "And I was so unkind to you on the whole of the Emigrant Road. Please, can you forgive me for that?"

Connor embraced her; his own eyes uncharacteristically misty. "I forgave you long ago, Georgie," he assured her. Then he drew back, his features solemn. "I've been thinking maybe we started out wrong," he said, taking both her hands in his. "I don't know what made me think I could just marry a stranger and expect her to love me in return without taking time to know her. These last six months with you, even though you were so distant in spirit, I learned to know who you are, and it made me love you more than I ever thought I could love a woman."

Gyorgyike blinked. She knew for a fact she had made herself as unlovable as possible, and yet Connor had somehow seen past all her walls.

"I want to marry you again," he said, squeezing her hands. "This time in front of a preacher instead of a magistrate. We're going to do this the right way." Suddenly, he slipped the ring off her finger and got down on his knees in front of her.

Gyorgyike felt herself blushing, but she didn't mind, even with an audience of wide-eyed children present. Gabor ran over to them and stared at Connor in curious wonderment, his gaze flitting back to his mother's face now and then.

"Gyorgyike Szarka, will you be my wife?"

A breathless hush hung over the group of emigrants gathered in the simple house.

Gyorgyike could feel her heart beating in her ears. She wanted to tell him she had also learned to love him through the hardships they had shared on the seemingly endless and yet breathtakingly beautiful trail, but there didn't seem to be words that fitted well enough. Except maybe the words she knew he was waiting to hear. "I will, Connor Slade. It will honor me to be your wife."

Connor's grin nearly wrapped all the way around his head. He slipped the ring back onto her finger, stood up, and helped her to her feet, then he embraced her. They stood that way while a cacophony of cheering and clapping and stamping of feet erupted all around them.

"A weddin'!" Billy yelled ecstatically. "First party in our new house is goin' t' be a weddin'!"

"Congratulations, Georgie and Connor!"

"Oh! What a wonderful surprise! For all of us, even you, Connor!"

"Should it be a winter wedding? Or maybe we should wait for spring when there are more wildflowers."

The questions and congratulations reverberated all around them, but there was only one thing Gyorgyike could hear. The beat of Connor's heart against her ear as the drum for a song she had heard Anna singing often while she went about her chores or trudged beside the prairie schooner.

*The Lord is my Shepherd, I'll not want, He makes me down to lie in pastures green, He leadeth me the quiet waters by.*

It was true. She could not possibly have imagined this kind of ending to her Emigrant Road, let alone conceived and planned and achieved it. It could only have been orchestrated by a higher hand. At once, she knew what her homestead would be called: Green Pastures.

At last, she was home.

The End

I hope you enjoyed this story.

I would appreciate a positive review on Amazon.

More Classic Westerns are in the works...coming soon.